An Unorthodox Match

by Patricia Bourque

This is a work of fiction. Names, characters, places and incidents are either the product of the author's imagination or are used fictitiously. Any resemblance to actual persons, living or dead, events or locales is entirely coincidental.

For Abe

"The mind is its own place, and in itself can make a heaven of hell, a hell of heaven.." John Milton, Paradise Lost

1964 -January, Montreal

David waved off his friend Marcel. Swiping the kippah off his head, he stuffed it into his coat pocket and ducked into Woolworths. Cupping his frozen hands to his mouth he exhaled warm moist air to will them back to life.

Smells of grease, damp wool clothing, the hum of dissonant voices and clattering dishes were becoming familiar to him – he still felt guilt, but it wasn't the paralyzing guilt he experienced the first time he dared drink from the non-kosher cup of black coffee. Easing himself on to the only available counter stool, he dropped his book bag onto the puddled terrazzo floor.

"Be right with you hon," the waitress said, quickly stacking washed cups and saucers.

Brushing snow off his right shoulder, he noticed the profile of the young girl on the stool next to him. Dark chestnut hair curled around her shoulders. Her lips were faintly moving along the line of the pocket-book novel she was engrossed in.

"What can I get ya hon?"

"Coffee. Black."

"That'll be 25 cents." She stowed the pencil behind her ear.

Pushing aside his winter coat, he reached his hand deep into his pants pocket feeling around for the change he knew he had, only he didn't. His fingers brushed the skin of his leg. Flushed with embarrassment he mumbled, "Um, I'm sorry, I seem to have lost my...ahhh..." He reached down to grab his bookbag off the floor.

"I'll get it." Removing the dollar bill the girl was using as a book mark, she placed it on the counter.

"Thank you Miss but you..."

"It's alright. Don't worry about it."

"I'll pay you back. I really do have a hole in my pocket." He started pulling the lining out of his pants. The waitress placed the change on the counter.

"I said, don't worry about it."

"Fine. But I'll pay you back."

"Not necessary."

Exasperatingly stubborn! She probably thinks I'm a pauper! After a pause he asked, "Do you come here often?"

Reluctantly, she turned down the corner of the page and closed the book. Swiveling on the stool she was surprised to see a pair of intense dark eyes in a handsome, young face.

"Sometimes after class. I'm taking a secretarial course across the street. It's bitterly cold out so I thought I would have something warm before I get into my freezing car. And you?"

"Me what?" He was taken aback by her directness, not to mention her arresting thick lashed brown eyes. He had very little experience interacting with girls, other than his sister, Ruth. In his world, girls were kept separate and study was your life. Even just being in Woolworth's was out of his comfort zone, but lately he had been having some unexplainable compulsions of wanting to venture out beyond his restricted enclave.

"...come to Woolworth's often?" she asked with a bemused smile.

"Ah, no."

"Alrighty then. Well, I've got to go." She said, pulling her coat around her, stuffing the book into her pocket and draining the rest of her cup.

"Wait! How can I repay you?"

"I told you, forget it." As an afterthought she asked, "you want a drive somewhere?"

"No...okay maybe, yes."

She had already turned and was striding toward the door.

Heads down they walked in silence against the freezing wind. Arriving at the red Valiant convertible, she unlocked the doors and David slid onto the rock hard faux-leather seats. The thin material of his coat was no defense against his freezing bum.

She can't be more than eighteen and she has a car? Here I am, twenty-two and still living at home.

He gave her directions. The car hadn't warmed up fully before she came to a stop in front of the three story tenement building on Clark street. Suddenly David felt something he had never experienced before – embarrassment for where he lived; and guilt for feeling embarrassed.

On impulse he wanted to give her his phone number, but there was no way he could explain a girl calling his house. *Or maybe I should ask her for her phone number. But no, for sure she's not…why start something I can't finish.*

"Thanks for the ride," he said, stepping out of the car. He didn't want it to be over, but he couldn't think of anything else to say.

"Hey! What's your name?" she asked abruptly.

"David." he said, bending his head back into the car.

"Byyye David," she said with a musical lilt and a mischievous grin on her face. She pulled away from the curb and he watched the red car disappear around the corner.

Jiggling his key into the keyhole of the scraped wooden door, he let himself into the main entrance and was hit by a blast of warmth and the smell of frying onions. Taking the stairs two at a time to the third floor, unconscious of the smile on his face, he opened the door to the kitchen of the cold water flat.

"Who was that?" Ruth accosted him before he even had time to remove his coat.

"What is it your business?" His older sister could be such a nudge. "A friend, do you mind?"

"It was a girl, wasn't it? I saw her from the window."

"A friend, a girl! What of it?"

"Why are you getting upset? I'm just asking. Because you know the Pa…"

"I know! Dammit, I know. You don't have to remind me!"

Chapter One

1969 – Five years later

"Hold him still Jace! He just kicked my seat. I'm gunna have an accident!"

"How do you expect me to get a grip on him! He's freakin' strong!"

Her head jerked back suddenly, "OW! He's eating my hair!"

"He's not eating your hair! I grabbed it trying to grab him! Shit! He stinks like hell! Whose idea was it to bring him in the car anyway? I don't know how you talked me into it. I'm choking from his smell! "

"Musk. Phew," she said, wrinkling her nose, "it is heavy though. I had to do it for Annie. I told you, she needs this buck for her flock."

"Flock schmock, I'll be lucky if I don't get gored in the gut," Jace grunted as he struggled to hold Basura by his horns. Bleating angrily, the billy goat reared up hitting the ceiling of the Chrysler New Yorker. Nervously, Jorie glanced at the wrestling match taking place in the rear view mirror. She hoped Basura hadn't put a tear in the ceiling fabric. *How will I explain that to my father?*

"Hang on. We're almost there. But don't let him jump out. Stay in the car until I see where she wants him. I told her we're coming."

"Oh yeah. Easy for you to say! At least roll down the freakin' windows so I can breathe. I'll never get this musk shit smell off."

As they pulled into the driveway of the farm, Annie was just coming out of the barn with a rope in hand. Jorie quickly put the car in park and jumped out.

Without waiting, Jace threw the back door open.

"Thanks so much Jorie. Hold on Jace – Let me loop this around his neck so we can lead him to the barn," Annie said, reaching into the back seat and sliding it over the bucks neck. "I've got a couple of does in heat and I don't want him...Jace! Grab the rope!"

Too late. The billy goat leaped over Jace and took off at a run. Jorie and Annie gave chase. Jace clambered out and stood by the car fastidiously brushing his clothes off and cursing under his breath. Suddenly the ram turned, reared up and charged him, butting him in the stomach and knocking him to the ground. Jace was not a small man, but he was no match for an angry goat's headbutt. Reaching for the rope, the girls fell into each other as the ram raced between them, quickly pivoting back. Jace, seeing the ram giving him the stink-eye as he reared up, scrambled to his feet, not quickly enough, as Basura knocked him down again and suddenly he felt something warm and sticky on him.

"Jesus! That goat just peed on me!" he yelled, as Basura nimbly jumped out of his reach.

"He's horny and smells the females" Annie said apologetically, grabbing the rope and yanking the goat away. "I'm so sorry Jace."

"Thanks for the warning…a little too late. Oh god, do I stink," he said shaking the pee off his hands and shirt. "Do you have any idea how expensive these clothes are?" He cursed loudly.

Annie yelled over her shoulder, leading the goat to another pen, "wash up in the barn – there's some towels. Jorie – thanks so much! Talk later."

"Thanks so much, hmph – fine for her; what about me? I'm a mess!"

"You'll be okay. I'll drop you off and you can take a shower."

"What about my $80.00 shirt? And these jeans! I don't know why I let you talk me into…"

Putting her finger on his mouth to shush him, she said, "because you love me, and you're the best," she planted a kiss on his cheek.

"Right now, that's very debatable."

"Oh stop. You know you love me."

Running some water over a towel in the stable, she proceeded to mop up his shirt.

"Here," he said, roughly snatching the towel from her hand. "Give me that. This water feels even worse. At least the piss was warm."

"While you do that, can I have two minutes to say hello to Mardi?"

Without waiting for his answer, she ran down the aisle to the stall with the wooden sign, 'Mardi-Gras', engraved in gold letters. Opening the stall door, she entered as the horse turned and nickered softly to her. Stroking his nose, she said, "How's my big beautiful boy? I know I've been neglecting you, but I promise it won't be much longer."

Two years ago her father had bought him for her as a birthday present on the condition that she pay for his upkeep herself. Even though it was costing a chunk of her salary to board him, she knew it was the best possible place and Annie had him exercised and groomed regularly. Luckily she was able to manage with the extra income she earned working at a discotheque on the weekends. Running her hand down his firm golden buckskin neck she inhaled his horsie scent, savoring it. He was in great shape.

"Jace," she yelled, "come and see how good Mardi is looking."

"You c'mon. We have to get back to the city," he hollered back grumpily.

Sighing, she kissed the horse on the nose and reluctantly left the stall.

***

On the half hour drive home, a decidedly uncomfortable and tense silence hung in the air.

"Can you slow down. You're driving way too fast. Slow down!"

"Like you don't drive your fancy sports car faster than this? Why are you being so crabby anyway? I have to take the car to the car wash before I give it back to my dad.

"First of all, I'm a much better driver than you are and second, SLOW DOWN! or let me out. I've had enough for today."

Maybe it wasn't the best decision I've ever made, transporting the goat in the car, but why can't Jace see the humor in it? So what if his clothes got dirty — he has tons of nice clothes. I hate it when he gets grumpy. And I can't stand the silence between us.

"Want to go to a movie this evening?" she asked, softening her voice. "Bonnie and Clyde is playing downtown."

"Not tonight. I told the boys I'd go out with them for a few drinks."

Oh, he's punishing me and I know what that means. When he went out with 'the boys', they drank too much and acted stupid and she often suspected he cheated on her.

"So they're more important to you than me?"

"Jorie, don't start up with something you can't finish."

"What does that mean?"

"It means that I'm going out with the boys and that's what it means, period."

"You're such an idiot Jace — you're twenty-five. When are you going to grow up?"

"Yeah, like you're the one to talk - with a goat in the car. I'll be lucky if they let me in the elevator stinking like this."

She hated it when they parted angry at each other but she knew there was nothing she could say that would change his mind. Pulling alongside the curb in front of his new luxury apartment building she turned her head away when Jace leaned over.

"No kiss then? Fine." He quickly opened the car door and exited, slamming it behind him.

Jorie wiped a tear as she pulled away. Jace was everything she ever wanted. Handsome, successful, supremely self-confident, charming, but faithful? She wasn't sure. There were just too many temptations for him and she was beginning to think now that he had her, the challenge was over.

Chapter Two

1969

Thursday - Champagne day at Gilly's Discotheque. A big ten cents a glass. Jorie and her girlfriends sat around the table laughing and sipping rotgut Champagne while the music thumped away. She worked at Gilly's Friday and Saturday evenings spinning the records and pretty much knew all the regular customers.

"Garçon, another round for me and my four friends," one of the tipsy girls yelled, motioning the waiter. She plunked down a whole fifty cents for the round of drinks, "and a fifty cent tip for you my fine young man." Franko, the waiter, looked at them cynically and rolled his eyes.

"Franko, you know we love you," Gloria slurred, reaching out and patting his arm.

Normally Jorie would be laughing along with the rest, but as much as she tried, she couldn't get in the mood and even the buzz from the four rounds of cheap champagne hadn't helped. She and Jace hadn't spoken since the goat fiasco. Today was already Thursday and she couldn't shake the feeling of anxiety. *What if he doesn't care for me anymore? He's probably having a great time with some other girl, fawning over her, using his charm to make her think she's the only girl in the world. Oooh, I just hate him. It's all my fault for doing stupid things. I'm such an idiot.* The alcohol wasn't helping. It was just bringing her down and making her brood.

Finishing their drinks, Vicky checked her watch. "It's only 8:30. Why don't we walk down the street and check out that great new band - they're from New York and already have hit records."

Jorie hadn't eaten since noon and was feeling more than light-headed as they strolled along busy downtown St. Catherine street, arm in arm to keep their balance.

"Look at those shoes," Jorie said, yanking back on the arms of the two girls. She swayed a bit as she gazed into the storefront window. "I think I need to buy a pair of those."

Hella dragged her past the store. "Just keep moving. You're in no shape to be buying anything right now."

"Aw, you're always looking out for me, my little friend," Jorie said sloppily.

"Well, somebody has to. You're such a cream puff, you'd end up getting squished if I didn't."

Outside the club where the New York band was playing a long line-up of people were waiting to get in. Assessing the five attractive girls, the bouncer signaled them to the front of the line ushering them past the velvet rope into the dimly lit interior. The club was garish with worn red carpeting, electric blue walls and a platform surrounding the stage with brown tables and chairs. A hazy cloud of cigarette smoke hung in the air. The band was rocking out some of their latest hits.

Seating them at a table adjacent to the stage, the girls ordered a round of drinks; Jorie opting for a soft drink. Returning with their order, the waiter said drinks were on the band and passed Jorie a folded note. Jorie noticed that the guitarist was looking in her direction with a very flirty, or was it hungry, look on his face. Opening the note, she read it, and passed it around the table.

We'd like you girls to be our guests at our hotel when we finish here at 1:00. We'll have a limo outside to take you. Sure hope you can join us.

Immediately there was a buzz of excitement among them. And all the while the band mates were looking at them eagerly while not missing a beat.

"Let's go!" Gloria said without hesitation. "They singled us out and they're really good looking – that drummer is yummy.

"Yeah, let's go – it'll be fun," Karen chimed in.

Vicky and Hella looked at Jorie who was starting to sober up.

"You girls can go if you like, but I'm not going. They're a band. What do you think they want us for? It's fun that they asked us and everyone in the club knows it, but let's leave it there."

The waiter was standing impatiently, shifting from foot to foot, waiting for a response from Jorie.

"I'm with Jorie. So, what's the decision?" Hella asked, looking around at the over-eager faces.

"I guess you're right," Karen groused.

"Well if you guys aren't going, I'm not going alone," Gloria chimed in with a pout.

The waiter, by now, bored with anticipation, handed Jorie his pen and she scribbled on the back of the note.

We're enjoying your music but unfortunately can't make it to the 'after-show'. Thanks for the invite.

She folded it over and handed it back to him. The whole second set the guitarist kept glancing at Jorie. At one point, he mouthed, 'pleease'. Jorie shook her head with a mock sad face.

That night in bed, she found herself thinking…Maybe we should have gone. Just for the fun experience… I can only imagine how jealous Jace would be…suppose I ended up in one of the tabloids being seen on the arm of the guitar player. On the other hand, twelve out-of-town guys who thought they were kings of the music world and five girls. The odds were not good.

***

The next morning at the office was torture. Hangovers from cheap wine are the worst, she groaned to herself. The florescent lights didn't help either as she made her way down the hall to the ladies room. Passing the mirrored wall over the sinks she glanced at herself, *good grief! I look like a vampire.* She dug around in her purse for some Erase and ran it over the dark circles under her eyes. *If I can just sit a few minutes and close my eyes, I'll feel better.* Closing the cubicle door, she sat down on the toilet seat and shut her eyes.

"OW!" she yelped, struggling to get off her knees in the small space. How long had she slept? She could already feel the bump rising where her forehead had connected with the metal door. *Just great. A vampire with a lump on my head. Why am I doing this to myself.*

***

By Friday, her resistance had worn thin. She hated herself for it as she dialed his number after work. Her heart beat faster hearing his phone ring. She wasn't sure what reaction to expect.

"Jace? Are you picking me up after work tonight?" she blurted out.

A pause…"I don't know, do you want me to?"
"I wouldn't have called you if I didn't, would I?" *Why does he always have to be so contentious. Make me feel 'less than' for giving in.*

"What do you need this job for anyway? Your old man has plenty of money. Friday and Saturday nights are when everybody goes out.."

So he's starting right in, she groaned to herself. *No 'how are you'? 'I was thinking about you'...crap! Why did I even call?*

"Unlike you, I'm not a trust fund baby. And just cuz my parents have money, doesn't mean I have. Besides, I need the extra money to support my horse and I want to move out and get my own place."

"Yeah, yeah, okay." His 'go-to phrase' to put a lid on anything he didn't like. This wasn't a new argument. Jace wanted her to be available when it was convenient to him.   "I'll be in around midnight"

"Why so late?"

"It's boring for me to sit around watching all the guys ogle you while you're working the records."

"They're just nice guys and there's no ogling. *Well, very little ogling,*" she chuckled to herself. *It isn't so bad to let Jace have some jealousy. But is he jealous or just too over-confident about me to worry?*

Hanging up the phone she slipped into a black and white checked mini dress, pulled on a pair of white go-go boots and went into the bathroom to finish her hair and make-up. Leaning close to the mirror and squinting one eye, she carefully applied the glue to an eyelash, 'these false eye-lashes were worth every dollar', she mumbled to herself setting the eyelash carefully in place. Pulling the sides of her hair up into a pony tail she fastened it with an elastic band brushing it out to blend with the cascade of dark chestnut hair. Lastly, she picked up her compact and swiped pink lipstick over her generous lips. Standing back from the mirror, she gave her eyelashes a flirty flutter.

Thinking about Jace coming to pick her up after work, she had taken extra care to look perfect, but sometimes she wondered if it all contributed to a superficiality in their relationship. There was no doubt in her mind that most of the attraction on his part was physical, but so was much of hers. *Would I still have the same feelings for him if he wasn't so handsome and charming? And the sports car doesn't hurt either. Oh pooh. Don't always overthink things. That's what he's always telling me when I get too serious.*

Arriving at the club before opening, she stowed her stuff in the back room and went to the record booth. On the turntable was an expensive bottle of perfume. A little note with a hastily scrawled message read, 'Love ya Baby. Your secret admirer'.

She was pretty sure she knew who her secret admirer was. Glancing around, she noted there was only her and two of the three owners in the empty club. One of them winked. She needed this job and wished he would stop coming on to her. So far she had managed to keep him at arm's length. Picking up the perfume she walked over to their table.

"Chad, did you leave this for me?" she asked holding the card and bottle out. "I'm afraid I have to return it. It's really thoughtful of you, but much too expensive for…"

"What makes you think it's from me?" he interrupted.

"Um… I just thought since it's only the three of us here, that you might have…"

"What does the card say? Why me? Maybe it's from Mike," he said, glancing at Mike who was benignly taking in the conversation with a stolid face.

Jorie was starting to feel uncomfortable standing in front of the two of them while they remained seated, legs casually stretched out, watching her squirm. Maybe she was wrong in assuming it was Chad. "I just meant…"

"I know what you meant. You think you're so hot that I would actually spend that kind of money to impress you?"

"Of course not." Jorie felt herself flush from embarrassment. "I'm sorry, but if you didn't leave it, who did? The cleaning people?"

"Okay Chad. Enough," Mike said suddenly standing up from his chair. "Own up and let's get this show on the road. It's time to open. It's alright honey. He's just afraid you're going to blow him off and damage his under-blown ego – keep the perfume. He can afford it." With that, they both got up and walked away.

Jorie went back to the booth unsure of what implications the whole discussion had. Maybe she should have just kept the perfume and her mouth shut. She certainly didn't expect such an aggressive reaction from Chad. And Mike was sitting there quietly laughing the whole time. It was humiliating.

There were several of the same regulars who always sat on the bar stools near her booth and flirted with her. They had stopped asking for dates after being refused so often but none of them had ever become aggressive. Sometimes they would bring her flowers, other times jewelry or once, one left a little book of love poems. The jewelry she returned but many times gifts were left anonymously. They were good for her ego, but she really wasn't interested. She was crazy about Jace. In some ways, she wished she had never met him.

She put a record on the turntable and thought back to how it was just over sixteen months ago at the advertising agency where she had started her first real job. He was already an account executive and she had been hired as secretary to the President of The Abbott Advertising Agency. Jace was everything a dream man could be. Tall, thick sandy hair, handsome and charming – unfortunately he was all too aware of his comely attributes. The office heart-breaker.

It didn't take long for him to zero in on the new girl. He was just a little too cocky, too smooth and too sure of himself; her instincts told her he would be trouble. Thanking him politely, she blew him off. After that, the chase was on. He pursued her relentlessly, even going so far as to force a deep kiss on her in the office kitchen. Stunned and unnerved by his aggression, she slapped his face, hard. Before she could blink, he slapped her back, across her breasts. Shocked, but against her own better judgement, she found herself amused by his originality and made the mistake of giggling. A month later they were an item. But now that they had been dating for over a year, she knew he was taking her for granted. The trouble with dating a hunk, was that other girls were always after him and if the man was inclined...

By eleven-thirty the club was packed. Putting another record on, Jorie danced out of the booth shaking a tambourine to the beat. A group of young people were coming in. Among them a smallish girl of about twenty-two wearing a pale blue mini skirt and matching jacket who stood out like a dazzling beacon. Long blonde hair, wildly frizzed, haloed her perfect sun kissed face. She had an ethereal glow about her. The girl began to dance wildly doing a strange repetitive movement with her arms and people fell back on the dance floor to give her room. Everyone was mesmerized. The dance wasn't lurid, just strangely primitive and innocently sexual. At the end of the record, she stopped and looked around as if she had come out of a trance. Shortly afterward, she and her party left. She was something alright and Jorie was glad that Jace wasn't there to see her. She hated that he always made her feel insecure.

Around midnight, unable to resist, she kept glancing towards the door until she saw him confidently stroll into the club. Greeting everyone as if he were a movie star he finally sauntered over to the DJ booth. Spotting the perfume on the shelf he frowned flashing her a quizzical look with a raised eyebrow.

Anticipating a sulk, she quickly said, "I don't know who it's from. Doesn't matter."

He glanced at the guys on the bar stools – they quickly turned their heads away as if they were deeply involved in a conversation.

"It's almost one. Do you feel like going to the Hawaiian Lounge when you wrap up here? I told Marcel we'd meet them there."

So it wasn't really a question. Like maybe are you too tired to go out after working all evening? Always his plans. "Sure, just let me put this stuff away and collect my money."

Sliding the bills into her purse, she sighed, relieved that he hadn't started a fight over the perfume. But then again, maybe he just didn't care that much.

***

The Hawaiian Lounge was a gay bar in the seedier part of town. All the cool straight kids frequented it to see and be seen. They had the best dance music in the city and some of the best acts as well.

Jorie blinked her eyes as she waded into the low hanging smoke. The packed crowd was a mix of butch women with ultra feminine girlfriends, mincing men holding their drinks and hunky guys checking the mincers out. A bar congested with hobnobbing people went up one side and at the far end was a stage barely visible through the haze of cigarette smoke with a band pounding out funky music.

Jace and Hella's boyfriend, Marcel, went across the room to speak to someone they both knew. Jace had left for another job shortly after Jorie started at Abbott Advertising but he had smoothly maintained his friendships with his colleagues.

Jorie and Hella tried to talk, but between the inhaled smoke and the loud music, Jorie's throat was beginning to dry up. She tilted the beer bottle to her lips. Hella tapped Jorie on the shoulder and pointed. Weaving her way through the crowded tables a tall, blonde, very fit, chiseled-faced lesbian in a white shirt and hip-hugging faded jeans was zeroing right in on Jorie. Charisma and confidence just oozed like a shield around her.

Putting her hand out, she asked in an awesomely sensual voice, "would you care to dance my lady?"

Jorie's mouth fell open. She was mesmerized until she saw Jace coming back through the crowd.

"Um, I'm sorry, ah, I, I can't right now, thank you."

Noting Jorie's eyes glancing past her, she nodded graciously as if quickly sizing up the situation and melted back into the crowd. Reaching her, Jace's mood changed quickly. He continued to pour on the charm with everyone else, but she knew he was angry and it put a damper on the whole atmosphere.

Driving on the way home, Jace sulked. "If I wouldn't have been there, you were going to dance with her, weren't you?"

"So what? We're in a gay bar you know. You don't get upset if I dance with Vicky or Hella or even Marcel or Jerry."

"That's different."

"Why is that different?"

"I saw the way you looked at her."

"I was just surprised that she asked me to dance. That's all. You know I'm straight all the way. But she *was* pretty hot." Jorie muttered this last under her breath.

"So why don't you just go out with your gay girlfriend!"

"I never even met her before! Stop yelling and acting like a fool. Grow up! Why are you so insecure? You have girls tripping all over themselves around you… do you see me get upset every time you pour on the charm?" Jorie gave a sigh of disgust.

A long silence ensued. The atmosphere in the car was suffocating.

"I need a break – I think it's time we took a break from each other."

"Fine with me," she replied through clenched teeth. "Or was that just the excuse you were looking for."

Jorie could feel the hot tears welling up and she didn't want to give him the satisfaction of seeing her cry. *Oooo. He is so infuriating. Sure, okay for him to flirt and probably cheat on me, but if someone looks at me cross-eyed…Stupid stupid man. Why did I ever fall for him! I should have known better.*

Jace pulled the sports car up to the drive-way of her parent's house. Jorie didn't even wait for him to stop, but jumped out slamming the car door and flounced up the walk-way. She didn't look back when she heard him peel away from the curb.

She was glad everyone was in bed. She ran into her room, put her face in the pillow and sobbed.

Chapter Three

The first week after she and Jace broke up had been miserable and she had to steel herself from giving in and calling him. She pictured him charming some other woman and having a great old time with his stupid immature friends while she moped around pining away. And for what? After the initial pursuit, when he finally had her hooked, she realized that he was more about the chase and less about the substance of the relationship. But, somehow she felt there was an attachment between them. He just wasn't mature enough to know how to sustain it. And she kept telling herself, he'll change. The greatest folly of women; she and her friends discussed the subject often. Women were always saying, 'I wish…' or 'I hope…' while men just went about their business and did whatever they pleased. She gave a big sigh just as her boss appeared at her desk.

"Apologies for interrupting your heavy thoughts, Jorie. I'd like you to meet David Kaisman, our new controller. David, this is Jorie-Anne Fielding, our much esteemed and valued secretary," Abbott said, with a kindly wink. "She'll be helping you get settled into your new office." Jorie stood up and offered David her hand.

"Hi David. Nice to meet you." Cocking her head and narrowing her eyes, she said, "you look strangely familiar to me."

"And you as well."

"I'll leave you two to figure out where you met. David, if you need anything, my door is always open. Welcome to the company."

"Thank you sir."

As Mr. Abbott walked off down the hall, Jorie turned to David.

"Maybe we've run into each other at a club?"

"I doubt it. I've never been to a club."

"Oh," she pulled in her chin in surprise. "Okay, well, I'm sure it will come to me – probably when I'm lying in bed at 1:00 in the morning," she said with a chuckle.

That fell flat.

I mean it wasn't the wittiest thing I've ever said but he could at least politely have laughed.

Bobbling her head, she rolled her eyes and turned abruptly starting down the hallway. "Let me show you to your office then."

Reaching for the brass handle of the custom walnut door, Jorie said, "Abbott Advertising is a great company to work for – I'm sure you're going to like it here. Everybody's very friendly, in fact, we do quite a bit of socializing together after hours." She couldn't seem to stop babbling.

David walked into the plush office, over to the window and looked out, then he glanced around the room. She studied him while he was studying the office and waited for a response. He had a rather prominent nose, well sculpted lips and eyes that were almost black under generous eyebrows. His features came together in a very attractive way, Jorie thought. The epitome of tall, dark and handsome.

"Isn't this a beautiful office David?" *Just go back to your desk already and shut up!* Instead, she waited. Feeling miffed at his lack of response, Jorie said dismissively, "Alrighty then, well, I'll let you get settled in. If you need anything, I'm just down the hall."

"Thanks."

Well, isn't he just Mr. Personality she hmphed to herself.

***

Three weeks and she hadn't heard from Jace and she was damned if she would be the first to call him. Some of the rawness was working itself out. Vicky asked if she was up for a club night at The Copa after work.

Walking down the street towards the club, Jorie laughed to Hella and Vicky, "We've got the market covered." Hella was a petit redhead, Vicky was a tall, slim model type blonde and Jorie was the curvy brunette.

She had called Frank to meet her outside the club. He worked for the sanitation department and wasn't the brightest bulb in the pack, but he was movie star good looking, a body builder, good natured, uncomplicated, and crazy about her. Whenever she needed a date in between her break-ups with Jace she called him. She felt a bit guilty for using him, but he didn't seem to mind and they looked great together.

The club was already in full swing. People were lined up along the stairs and onto the street waiting to get in. Rudy, the bouncer spotted them. He motioned with two fingers to come to the front of the line.

Frank was thrilled to be seen with the three attractive girls and after they were seated and ordered drinks, she and Frank stepped onto the stage to dance. From the higher elevation she had a good look over the floor and in a corner she spotted Jace with a beautiful, exotic looking girl. They were in an intimate conversation – she knew about Jace's intimate conversations. He had a way of making you think you were the only girl in the world and you were the only two in the room. Her heart about stopped. She didn't know if she was crushed or furious. *He is such a jerk. So immature!* Jace glanced up at the stage and their eyes locked. He gave her a down-turned look and shook his head, just barely, as if to say, you're trying way too hard or I'm disappointed in you. Jorie didn't know which, but how dare he insinuate anything about what she was doing. She turned away and gave the dancing her all, smiling and laughing at Frank, who had no inkling of the drama going on as he pulled her towards him for a brief kiss.

The next time she dared look, she saw Jace and the girl leaving thru the exit. *Good!* She hoped he was as upset as she was – but somehow, she felt he wasn't. Back at the table, she told Hella and Vicky and ordered another beer. After that and several more drinks, everything became a blur.

***

Work the next day was barely tolerable. She could hardly keep her eyes open. She really liked her job at Abbott but she was going to blow it if she kept on partying. Closing her eyes, she must have dozed off sitting up.

Jarred awake by the ringing phone, she heard Jace's voice when she picked it up. Her heart did a flip-flop. She could kick herself for having that reaction to his voice. He asked if she was free at lunchtime and could he pick her up to talk. *Talk is the right word.* She wasn't interested in having sex just because maybe he didn't get it from last night's girl.

Hanging up the phone she noticed David standing in the doorway watching her.

"Sorry, I didn't mean to eavesdrop. I wonder if you can tell me where to find the financial records for the Candyman campaign."

They had barely exchanged words since he had come to the job. He either had no personality or a mystery life. She chose to think he was a mystery, one she was determined to unravel and that was one area she knew she had the skills. She was a good listener and people were always dying to tell her their whole life story if she let them. He shouldn't be very difficult to crack if she put in some effort and turned on the charm.

She stepped around her desk and walked over to another small room. "They're over here David. In this closet along the back wall."

"Thanks."

Thanks? That's it? I don't think so. "So David, tell me about yourself," she asked in her most practiced casual voice. "You don't go to clubs or socialize, so what is it you like to do?"

"Mostly I study."

Study? Well, that sounds pretty boring. "Do you live at home?"

"Yes," he said, his back turned to her as he shuffled through the files.

What does that mean? Yes, your own place, or home with mommy and daddy? I should have phrased that question better. Hmmm, this is going nowhere. Maybe he's just obtuse.

"Do you have a girlfriend?"

He turned to look at her. The corner of his mouth gave way to a wry smile and a warning eyebrow lifted. "That's pretty personal, don't you think?"

Ignoring the insinuation, she continued, "I play the records at a discotheque down town on Friday and Saturday nights. Maybe you'd like to come and meet up with me and some of my friends?"

"Maybe I'll come one Saturday."

"What about this Friday? It's always busy. You'll have a good time."

"No, thanks." His tone was dismissive and final.

I knew it, I was too pushy. Ach. What a boring person. That's it. I'm not saying another word to him unless it's about business.

She left him in the room annoyed and puzzled. Usually men fell all over themselves to talk to her. Men, go know, she sniffed to herself.

***

David watched from the second floor window as the flashy sports car pulled into the Abbott parking lot. Jorie got into the passenger seat and they sped off.

She's a funny girl. Nosy or just inquisitive? Doesn't seem to have a care in the world except having fun. Very pretty though. How does one get to be so carefree? It would be interesting to spend some time with her, but I think she's more than I could handle. Besides why start something I can't finish. I could just imagine introducing her to my parents. 'Jorie-Anne? What kind of a name is that?'.

David shuddered. He was so tightly bound to his upbringing, the very thought of going against it gave him anxiety. And yet, if he was honest, he envied these young men and women who knew what fun was. They laughed easily. He couldn't remember the last time he or his family had laughed. They were a very sober bunch. He understood why, but at the same time, he would like to feel that he had at least a choice. Maybe after he got to know Jorie better, he would open up a little, but what if she was repulsed or worse…taking this job had been a risk for him. He had explained how he needed to leave early on Friday's during the short days and on certain holidays he couldn't come to work at all. It would have been easier going to work for a Jewish owned firm. The opportunity had been there, but something pushed him to go beyond his comfort zone and take this job. They had agreed to his terms without question, thanks to the glowing referrals he had received from his school and his one previous job, and welcomed him into the company. Well, time would tell.

The silence in the car was awkward. Finally Jorie could stand it no longer.

"Where are we going…?"

"To my place so we can talk."

"We can talk just as well in the car. And besides, I only have an hour and what is there to talk about? Seems from what I saw last night at the club, you've made up your mind about us."

"That girl? She doesn't mean anything to me. She's been coming on to me for weeks."

"If she doesn't 'mean anything to you', why go out with her?" Suddenly she had an upset stomach and started to hiccup.

"Why did you go out with that big bruiser?"

"Frank is just a good friend." Her stomach rumbled and she let out a loud spasmodic hiccup.

"He didn't look much like a friend to me."

"Okay, so where are we going with this 'discussion'." Hiccup. "I want something more serious, but if you keep flying off the handle every time somebody looks at me or worse, hiccup, cheating on me," she said through clenched teeth, "I don't think we have much of a future." Hiccup.

"Would you stop that noise PLEASE! I never cheated on you."

"You're such a liar Jace." Hiccup – her stomach jumped. "Maybe you're right, it would be best if we took a break from each other."

"Stop hiccupping for god's sake – it's so annoying!"

"Like I'm doing it on purpose just to annoy you. Maybe I have an upset stomach Hiccup from you screaming at me."

"I wouldn't be screaming if you stopped that annoying sound. So, there is somebody else – that Frank guy?" Jorie could see the argument was pointless.

"Nobody else." Hiccup. "I just don't want to fight all the time. Especially over nothing. Take me back to the office." Hiccup.

As he pulled into the parking lot, she jumped out slamming the car door behind her. *Ha! He hates it when anyone slams the door on his precious car.* She didn't look back as Jace hotly drove off the lot. *I was just feeling better about the break-up, but seeing him brought up all the mixed feelings again. He's such a magnet for me…but why? Sure he's handsome and cool but…but what else has he got? He's a playboy and he's not going to change for me.*

***

The office was divided into two sections; the main part where most of the staff worked, along with a small kitchen, and beyond the double polished wood doors, the inner sanctum with Mr. Abbott's office, Jorie's cubicle and the office for the controller. Stopping by the kitchen, she poured herself a cup of coffee and drank a glass of water to try and stop the hiccups. Walking the length of the office, she noted Hella and Vicky's empty desks. *They must have gone out for lunch — I should have gone with them instead of with that stupid, annoying man.* Pushing open the brass handle of the big wooden door she stepped onto the plush carpeting. Her mind was still reeling from the fight with Jace as she angrily plunked down the coffee cup on her desk. Spotting a dollar bill tucked under the stapler she saw David disappear down the hall.

Quickly following him, she stuck her face around the edge of his office door.

"David. Did you leave this dollar on my desk?" she asked, waving it in the air.

He smiled, a brilliant smile, and in a flash, it changed his whole demeanor.

"I remembered why you looked so familiar. Five years ago you paid for my coffee at Woolworth's. I said I would pay you back and now I did."

"Oh my gosh, you're right! I remember now. But here. You don't have to pay me back," she said, placing it on his desk.

"I insist…it's only 25 cents with interest. And at the time, you saved me from a great deal of embarrassment."

Walking back to her desk, she couldn't stop thinking about his dazzling smile. Maybe there is a human being in there, she thought.

Later that afternoon, the office was hushed. The only sound, the humming of the florescent lights. Sitting at her desk, she found herself thinking about David. She could have sworn she saw points of light gleam off his white teeth. He and Mr. Abbott had gone to a meeting downtown. A pile of work sat on her desk waiting to be transcribed and the quiet meant she would be able to get it done without being disturbed. With a sigh she inserted the Dictaphone earplugs and turned to the typewriter and began banging away at the keys.

Suddenly, from behind, a pair of hands covered her breasts and a husky voice said, 'guess who?' Jumping up so fast she knocked the steno chair over she turned to see Stan Johnson, the top sales rep, leering at her.

"What are you doing!" Her heart was racing and heat rushed to her face. "Get AWAY from me!"

Stan, with his greasy hair and mouth puckered into a tight, wrinkled little circle like an asshole, showing no sign of embarrassment on his face, had backed up casually blocking the only entrance. The cubicle of her office wasn't large. She pushed herself against the farthest wall gaging her chances of getting out the door.

"Where's Abbott…and that new guy? I went thru the office. It's empty. Looks like just you and me holding down the fort, babe," he said with a wolfish smile.

"They'll be back any minute", she stammered, knowing that wasn't true. There was no point in yelling for the girls in the main office. They wouldn't hear her through the heavy doors.

"So Jorie," he said, taking a step towards her. He reached down and set her chair upright still blocking her escape, "what are the chances of you and me getting better acquainted?"

She had no answer for that. Her mind was blank with panic.

He took a step towards her.

"Get away from me!"

"Calm down, baby. I just want to ask you a question." Another step closer. "What's your opinion on oral sex? You likee or you no likee?" He glanced back through the open door to the hallway.

Jorie's mouth had gone dry. She swallowed. Stan was staring hard at her. He seemed to be getting excited by her fear.

Suddenly feeling like a deer caught in the sights of a rifle, she lunged past him. He grabbed her arm but she yanked it free and ran into Mr. Abbott's office, into his private bathroom and locked the door.

Knocking on the door he tried a softer tactic. "Jorrrie, you can come out now. I mean it, c'mon out babe. I won't touch you. I was just foolin' around. You can take a joke can't ya?" He rattled the door knob. "C'mon pretty girl – I meant no harm."

Completely shaken, she sank down onto the toilet seat and tried to calm her breathing. Several minutes later, she put her ear to the door and heard him walk away. But did he leave, or was he waiting in the hallway? Fifteen minutes went by before she unlocked the bathroom door and tentatively stepped out. Quickly she walked down the hall through the walnut doors to the main office where Hella and Vicky worked.

"What's the matter? You look white as a ghost?" Hella said.

"Did you see Stan Johnson leave?"

"Yeah, five minutes ago. Did he make a play for you?" Vicky asked. "He's such a pig, always groping us and hugging us so he can feel our boobs against him. I told Mr. Abbott once and he did call him out, but he's the number one sales rep so 'he ain't goin' nowhere. Easier to replace us than him."

"Here," Hella said, pulling up a chair, "sit with us if you're still nervous – God! It's like a jungle out there with all these gorillas trying to jump us."

Vicky came over to commiserate with them. "Do you want some tea or a glass of water?"

"No, I'll be okay. That asshole jerk grabbed my boobs." Her hands were shaking as she tried to calm herself down.

"Remember last Christmas? When that old guy cornered you in the lady's room?" Hella asked. "Can you imagine? In the lady's room? Is nowhere sacred anymore?"

"How can I forget it...the horny old geezer was stronger than he looked – ick, he was so disgusting. Rotten smelly teeth and yellow fingers," Jorie grimaced even thinking about it.

"He was always fawning over us...saying what lovely girls we were," Hella sneered. "Lucky it wasn't me he tried that on. I would have kicked him in the balls but good. You're too timid Jorie. You need to toughen up. These jerks look for easy prey. Me, they won't dare tangle with."

Hella was petit, but she was a fast thinker, tough for her size and had a mouth to go with it. Most men tended to take a wide berth around her. Except Marcel. He seemed to have some deep understanding of her and there was no doubt he had found a soft spot in her heart. And Jorie too. She couldn't imagine having a better or more loyal friend.

***

For some reason David couldn't get Jorie out of his mind. *She has a boyfriend – that guy with the sports car I saw her with. Probably the same one that sends her the flowers she has on her desk every week.* He certainly had no intentions of getting into a competition but he couldn't seem to let it – her, go either. For the life of him, he couldn't fathom why he had the impulse to step out of his comfort zone and go against everything he had been taught and grown up with. He had seen it happen with some of his friends and it always ended up bringing the roof down on their heads and the consequences were not pleasant. It usually meant expulsion from the community and everything familiar. Friends and most everyone in the family were forced or chose to turn against you. *So, why do I want to risk it all?* He answered his own question. *Because I want to be free to explore and feel and think, differently – make my own decisions, not have them proscribed to me.*

And there she was, Jorie, the same irresistible compulsion that had driven him to take the job at Abbotts.

Chapter Four

Jorie tried to cover the shock on her face. The mute man was asking her to go out to lunch? *I suppose I'll have to do all the talking judging from our previous 'non-conversations'.*

They crossed the street and went to an Italian eatery close to the office. David couldn't imagine what he would order. He had never eaten in a non-kosher restaurant before. Pizza would be the safest thing.

The restaurant was quaint with checked tablecloths and the requisite table decoration, a straw wrapped Chianti bottle with candle drippings down the sides. Jorie was determined not to probe this time. *He can talk or not, I don't care, I'll just enjoy my food.* He ordered a plain pizza and when she ordered the peperoni pizza she noticed he grimaced.

"You don't like pizza?"

His face flushed. "No, it's not that."

"Well, what then? You're a vegetarian?" She smiled at him so he wouldn't think she was mocking him.

"No, it's just in my religion, we don't mix meat and dairy products." There, he said it and now he was waiting for her reaction.

"Ah, so you're Jewish. I thought so. Hella is Jewish, so I know a little bit about – but her family doesn't practice. Is it nauseating to you?"

"No, it's just not something I'm used to seeing."

"You're a mixed meat and dairy virgin."

She saw the expression on his face and knew she had been too cavalier with her comment. Mentally she kicked herself. He finally opened up about something and she shot him down.

"I'm sorry David, I apologize, I didn't mean to be insensitive. I have what you call 'foot in mouthitis.' Speak first, shut mouth after." *Great, now he'll never talk.*

"That's alright. I expect reactions like that. I have to admit this pizza is very good."

"Phew! Great. I'm glad." She pantomimed wiping sweat off her brow. "We'll have to come here again sometime." *Well, that was nice and forward. He seems so bound up, so controlled. It makes me nervous. And then I babble. I wonder what it would take to make him laugh out loud? Maybe he's never even laughed out loud. That would be sad.*

Just before closing the next day, Jorie knocked on David's door to drop off some typed documents.

"Oh, I'm sorry. I didn't mean to interrupt." She was taken aback to see a tailor on his knees pinning David's pant legs as he stood on a stool. There were books of fabrics strewn on his desk and more fabric samples on the chair. She had to admit he was a spiffy dresser in his three piece suits, but it never occurred to her that he had his suits made. *What a strange guy, not strange, but different. And that obviously new car, the huge maroon Ford Galaxy — that's something my father would buy, not a young guy. Hhmph.*

"That's alright Miss. I'm about finished. It will just take me a minute to pack up."

Hurriedly throwing the samples and swatches into a suitcase, the tailor quickly packed up his bag, stuffing his notes into his pocket and left.

"David, I don't suppose I could ask you for a favor? I bought a car. Would you be able to drive me there after work to see if it's ready."

She couldn't believe how forward she was. Hella or Vicky would gladly have taken her. *I mean the guy is hardly my friend after all.* But for some reason, she had a bizarre urge to spend more time with him.

Jorie could hardly sit still — driving through traffic in silence had her squirming in her seat. *He seems so at ease sitting there not saying a word. What's the saying? Still waters run deep. Yikes, I must be very shallow.* Glancing at his focused profile she studied his face and wondered what he was thinking? She was determined not to be a probing chatter-box and if he didn't speak, well, she would show him she could also not talk. But there was soooo much she wanted to know!

They entered the seedier part of town and pulled up to a five story garage building. David frowned.

"Did you buy it through a private sale?"

"The newspaper ad didn't say…it just said a Chevy II in running condition and gave this address."

"Well, let's go see…" he said, apprehensively.

They entered through a door on the side of the building into a squalid, dingy office. Sitting at a desk, a wiry, ferret-faced man in his twenties, garbed in a stained t-shirt and well-worn black pants jumped up. He eyed them both suspiciously.

"I'm here to pick up my car." Jorie pulled the ad out of her purse and handed it to ferret face. She noticed the fingernails on his dirty hands were bitten to the bloody quick.

"Your name and the number we gave you when you called."

She handed the information to him.

David was observing this with incredulity written all over his face.

"Follow me." Ferret-face took off at a good clip through the cavernous building. Up narrow metal stairs, around a corner, more stairs and down a row of cars.

"There it is," he said pointing.

"Where?" Jorie looked around.

"That one, the third one on the pile. The green one." "You mean the one on *top* of the other two cars?" asked Jorie, her eyes widening with surprise.

"Yep. All we need is your final payment. It's gonna take a few days to get it checked out and then it'll be all yours," he said, licking his lips and studying them both intently with hooded eyes.

David looked at Jorie to see what she was thinking. He was both stunned and fascinated. He could never imagine something like this taking place.

"Jorie, can I see you over here for a moment. Give us a minute alone," he nodded toward the guy while dragging Jorie by the arm.

"You can't buy a car from this guy. He's a shyster."

"But I gave him a $200.00 deposit."

David was shaking his head – *this girl is like a babe in the woods.* "It doesn't matter. Whatever car you're going to get isn't...did you talk to your father before doing this?"

"David, I'm not a kid. I don't have to ask my father."

"I think you do. Look, forget about the deposit. Let's just get out of here and I'll help you find a more suitable car."

"But…"

"No buts – let's get out of here before we get mugged." He was pulling her towards the stairs.

The salesman came scurrying over. "What's the problem?"

"She's changed her mind. I suppose there's no point in asking for her deposit back?"

"She owes us the rest of the $800.00. She signed a contract."

"You signed a contact?" David asked wide-eyed.

"They said I couldn't have the car without signing the contract."

"Please don't tell me." David turned to the man and said, "so sue her. You're going to lose. I'm her witness and I'll testify to what a schlock outfit you're running here."

The salesman scurried around to cut them off from the stairs. "Okay, here's what I'm going to do for you. I'm going to guarantee all the repairs for one year after you take possession of the car."

"David, that sounds like…" Grabbing her arm again, David, who was at least a head taller than the punk, pushed him aside and pulled Jorie towards the iron steps. The salesman went ballistic. "Yeah, see you in court you assholes and you're gonna lose big time."

Jorie looked back over her shoulder. "David, ow, you're hurting me. I don't want to be sued!" she said plaintively.

"Keep walking – you're not going to get sued. They're out and out crooks."

They emerged onto the street with the sleazy salesman hot on their heels spewing heated threats.

"Get in the car. I'll give you a lift to your place."

On the ride home, David gave her a lecture about being more cautious dealing with people.

"Didn't you have a red Valiant when I first met you at Woolworths?"

"That was five years ago! You remember that car? I did, but my brother borrowed it and smashed it in an accident. After that my father said we had to buy our own cars."

When they pulled up in front of her house, David was surprised to see how grand it was. His heart sank. *She's definitely out of my league, even if I had ever considered...*

"Thanks for the lift and I guess I should thank you for not letting me waste more money. Would you come in and say hello to my parents for a few minutes?"

Everything in him screamed Nooooo! Turning to her he asked, "You know I'm Jewish right?"

"And...so?" She pulled in her chin with a perplexed look. "My parents don't care about that."

I hope not.

She unlocked the front door. A small wild-haired dog came running to greet them, spinning joyous circles over and over.

"This is Catdog David. I found him in the country three years ago, half-starved and injured. He's a great little poochie, aren't you Catdog." She opened her arms and the dog trustingly leaped into them.

They stepped into a large foyer with black and white checked marble tiles. It was a beautiful house. He thought back to five years prior when she had dropped him off at the tenement building. He followed her into the living room. *What the hell is that?*

His eye was immediately caught by a dead rodent laid out in what looked like a miniature silver coffin, on the long credenza by the wall.

Jorie saw his surprised look. "That's my hamster, Hamlet, he passed away yesterday and I bought this little silver, red velvet lined, jewelry box at Woolworths. I thought it looked like a perfect hamster coffin. I had him almost four years. He was very sweet." David noticed her eyes mist over. "I'm going to have a little funeral for him this evening – can you imagine David, maybe hundred's of years from now, archeologists will dig him up and finding the tiny bones in this little coffin will wonder if he was worshiped as a god or something?"

David laughed at the sentiment, but could only shake his head in puzzlement at her vivid imagination. She didn't realize in the moment how happy it made her to see him laugh.

Footsteps in the hallway caused him to turn and he braced himself for the introduction. Her parents were much younger than he expected. *Big difference in age compared to my parents who are in their sixties.* Her father was tall and jaunty looking and her mother was, David thought, well taken care of.

"Mum, Dad, this is David Kaisman. We work together at the office. He gave me a ride home."

Pleasantries were exchanged all around.

"David, we were just sitting down to dinner. We would love it if you would join us," Mrs. Fielding asked.

Jorie saw David's cheeks color. "Mum, maybe David has another engagement."

"No, that's alright. I'd be pleased to join you."
Jorie glanced at David, impressed. God, I hope we're not having ham, she thought.

"Come, let's sit down," Mrs. Fielding said, leading the way to a charmingly appointed dining room. David glanced around at the artwork on the walls. He tried to relax. *It's only food. Not kosher, but still, only food.*

The Fieldings went into the kitchen and returned with salads and a large bowl of pasta Bolognese.

"Help yourself David," Mr. Fielding said. "We don't stand on formalities here."

David's heart pounded. Salad he could manage, but the meat sauce... His stomach was churning. MEAT – what kind? NOT KOSHER – TRAIF, kept playing over and over while he tried to carry on a conversation.

"David, what do you think of my sauce? It's a special recipe – lot's of red wine. Here, have some parmesan cheese. "

"Dad, David is Kosher. He can't..."

"Jorie," David said firmly, in a cautioning voice that told her he would take care of himself. "Thank you," he said taking some pasta from the edge of the bowl where the sauce barely touched. "It's very...rich, good," David swallowed hard. "Delicious." *If I can just keep my stomach from heaving.*

Jorie kept eyeing David. She felt bad for inviting him in knowing he was totally out of his comfort zone, although she had to give him credit, nobody else would have known. Her parents were totally unaware and kept the conversation flowing. At one point, Jorie's brother Rick came in from playing hockey and joined them at the table. The conversation quickly turned to Rick and the hockey game.

David seized it as his chance. "Excuse me, I'd like to use the bathroom?"

Sitting on the toilet letting his stomach settle he looked at the luxurious bathtub – he could never picture chickens in this bathtub.

After dinner, he thanked them and said he had to take his leave using the excuse he had some paperwork to do before morning.

Jorie walked him to the door. "I think that was very difficult for you, but you handled it brilliantly. I hope you're not going to go to hell now," she said with a weak smile. Leaning up, she gave him a kiss on the cheek.

After he drove away, he thought about the whole situation. It was so far out of his comfort zone, but he had survived the food and they hadn't asked him to leave. *She gave me a kiss on the cheek* – he could still feel her lips there. *She's a strange girl. Life would never be boring with her. But my life and hers…Well, that's got to end.*

Chapter Five

Jorie noticed she had been thinking less and less about Jace and more and more about David. David had something about him that Jace didn't, but she couldn't quite put her finger on what it was. David was definitely more serious – there was something deep about him that Jace was lacking. He had a strange combination of strength and fragility that Jorie found herself intrigued with.

In the office, the next morning, she went looking for him to see if he had anything to say about the night before. He was pouring himself a cup of coffee in the kitchen.

"Good morning," she chirped.

"Good morning," he said, while adding a teaspoon of sugar to his cup.

Washing the spoon, he placed it in the dish drainer and walked away. Jorie was deflated. She had been so excited to hear what he had to say, but this? And besides, she had spent extra time on her make-up and clothes for the biggest annual birthday party of the year at Candyman's and was it too much to expect a compliment at least?

Walking down the hallway towards his office, she told herself, *just let it go. Maybe he's in a bad mood or something.* But it wasn't her nature 'to let things go'. Oh no, she had to attack the problem head on, often to her own detriment.

His door was open. Knocking lightly on the door jamb, she entered his office. Before he could speak, she blurted out, "you're angry, aren't you? Because of eating stuff you shouldn't – you didn't want... I'm really sorry about even asking you to come in. I didn't think..." *and I'm off and babbling.*

"Jorie, stop! I'm not mad and not upset. Your parents were very gracious. After I left I just realized how different our worlds are. I don't fit in yours and you certainly don't fit in mine. That's all."

"That's all?" Completely puzzled, for once Jorie was speechless. She heard Hella calling her name from down the hall.

"We're leaving for the party. Are you ready? Mr. Abbott's taking four of us in his car," she yelled.

"So, I'll see you at the Candyman party?" Jorie asked David hopefully.

"I'll be there a bit later."

"You have to come. He's our biggest client, you know."

"I know," he said with a faint smile.

Crestfallen, she walked down the hallway to the main office. *This won't do. I'm not going to moon over a guy who obviously doesn't want to have anything to do with me — whatever his reasons are. Too bad for you David.*

As they entered the factory by the warehouse door, the music was blasting away and the heady smell of chocolate and every other sweet scent imaginable almost knocked her over. To the left of the gleaming stainless steel vats and spotlessly clean factory machinery, a large glassed-off section had been gayly decorated with balloons and streamers, huge fake plastic candies hung from the ceiling and bowls were piled high with every type of sweet imaginable. Colorful printed bags lay on the tables to be filled with candy to go. A huge banner at the back of the room read, 'Happy Birthday Andrew'. Hella poked Jorie and whispered, "that banner should really read, Happy Birthday Randy Andy, you lecherous old fart." They both laughed heartily at that.

A hundred and fifty top advertising people were milling around in groups at little tables. Jorie spied Stan Johnson across the room holding a drink in his hand. He winked at her. She glared back. He wasn't going to intimidate her here with so many people around. *Best just to keep an eye on him and stay away.*

After she had reported the incident to Mr. Abbott, although he hadn't fired Johnson, which would have been the best revenge, he had installed a key pad on the doors to the inner office so you could no longer just walk in without knowing the code. That gave Jorie some measure of satisfaction.

In the center of the room was a huge rectangular table laden with cold cuts, salads, breads of every sort and at one end, a chef carving tender roast beef alongside covered chafing dishes with delicious smells wafting off them. Wait staff were winding their way through the crowd with platters of delectable hors d'oeuvres. The open bar was a bee-hive of activity. Under the birthday banner was a huge cake decorated with jewel-like gumdrops and sparkles. Advertising people of all types and in all styles of clothing were clustered in cliques. The creative people with their funky hairstyles and get-ups, laughing and dancing to the music. The suit men. Staid, conservative, all business, even at a party.

Jorie sighed to herself – she couldn't stop thinking about David. *Oh pooh on him. I don't even really know him.* Get over it you fool, she thought, popping a dark chocolate almond into her mouth. Andrew Candy was their biggest client. Last year the party had been wild…too much liquor for everyone had fueled some embarrassing incidents between Candyman's staff and Abbotts and everyone was warned to be on their best behavior this year. Jorie reached for a glass of champagne from the waiter's tray as he passed by.

On the other side of the room, Hella was flirting outrageously with one of the Abbott boys home from college. There was no chance she would ever cheat on Marcel, but she liked to flirt… 'lure them in and then crush them,' was her revenge philosophy. Bradley Abbott was attractive, Jorie had to admit, with his tousled blonde hair and muscular build, but he was a spoiled and indulged brat as far as she was concerned. Jonathan, Bradley's older brother who worked as head of accounting at Candyman, was tall and sinewy with a pinched face like his father, but the few company dealings she had with him, she found him to be rudely condescending and arrogant. Neither one had any appeal for her.

She saw David arrive and the room immediately lit up. She watched him over in a corner talking to a man she had never seen before. Lost in thought over his coolness towards her that morning, she suddenly realized Mr. Candy was zeroing in on her. He was half soused, that was plain to see.

"Jooriee," he slurred, much too close as sour breath hit her in the face. The veins in his nose were Rudolph red and big fleshy pouches hung under his eyes. "Come my dear, I have something important to show you. Come, come," he said seizing her by the wrist and pulling her along. *Biggest Abbott client, biggest Abbott client, better go see. What can he have that I could possibly find 'important'? Oh god!"* Glancing over her shoulder she caught Hella's eye and grimaced.

He had a powerful grip for a skinny man. Leading her into his office and faster than a viper, he kicked the door shut behind him, put out his foot and tripped her onto the deep plush carpet. In two seconds he was on top of her.

"Mr. Candy! Get off me!" His hands were all over her fumbling with her panties and trying to get into her pantyhose. He was grunting like a pig. She hit him on the side of the head, hard, and that seemed to stun him for a second. Her heart was pounding. For sure I'll be fired for this, she thought trying to push the weight of him off her. There was a knock at the door. He stopped fumbling enough to listen just as Hella entered and without pause, stepped over his legs to stand beside him. Jorie scrambled away and got to her feet hastily smoothing her clothing.

Looking down at him on the floor, Hella scolded him. "Mr. Candy, what are you doing, you naughty naughty man. I told you last year that this was not acceptable behavior for someone of your status." He sat upright on the carpet and looked up sheepishly at her.

"What would your wife say if she had caught you, instead of me?" Hella shook her head making a disparaging noise, "tsk, tsk, tsk. C'mon Jorie, this particular party's finished." She grabbed Jorie by the arm and slammed the office door behind her.

Re-entering the party room, Jorie, flushed, continued to straighten her clothes and pulled her high pony tail tight. "Do you think Mr. Abbott will fire me when that pervert tells him I hit him?"

"Well, let's see. I can just hear 'jerkoff-face pervert' explaining to Abbott about why you hit him. Don't worry about it. He'll keep his yap shut. Let's go get a drink."

Walking toward the bar, Jorie's composure sank as she saw Jace walk in. She shuddered still feeling creepy Candy's hands groping her. *What did I do that gave him the impression I was that kind of girl?* She felt so dirty. Jace, however, looked amazing and his usual confident self as he strolled into the room. He glanced at David and Jorie froze hoping that he wouldn't start anything. Fortunately he quickly became distracted as several young stenographers rushed over to flirt with him. After making small talk and letting them fawn over him, he turned and came towards her. Jorie wasn't ready to face another assault, verbal or otherwise.

"Hi gorgeous. I was hoping to find you here," he said, his voice silky smooth and inviting. Taking her hand possessively under his elbow he led her over to a secluded corner of the room. "I've missed you and I've been thinking that maybe we can work things out if you want to give it a another try." Here was another man trying to lead her to where he wanted her to go. A knot of anger was forming deep inside her chest.

"Another try? Really Jace? When did I give you the impression that I'm a yoyo? Somebody on a string you can just reel in and throw out at whim? Did you even think to ask if I've missed you? Or maybe if I've already met someone else? Or even how I am?"

He gave a bemused smile as if he was indulging a child. "Well, it's plain to see that you look really fine and I don't see any particular guy next to you so I think it's safe to assume..."

"Don't assume anything Jace. You know nothing about me. You never did."

"Okay, why are you being so touchy today? That time of month?"

"You are such an idiot. Go play with the steno-pool."

"Don't be childish Jorie. You know what we had together, we understood each other and I don't think that's something you get over so easily. Or at least I don't."

"Childish? You think I'm being childish?" she shrieked – her nerves already on edge.

"Keep your voice down. You're causing a scene."

"Don't tell me to keep my voice down. I'll scream if I like! I'm sick of all you men thinking you can just do whatever you like. You're so full of yourself Jace. I think I'm pretty aware of where we stand."

"Men, what men are you talking about? Jorie? Tell me. You're not talking about that guy over there?" Making a disparaging face, he indicated David with his head.

"Oh please, just shut up and leave me alone. Don't even pretend you care about anyone except yourself."

Turning her head away so Jace wouldn't see the tears starting to pool, she saw David across the room staring pensively at them.

"I can't take it anymore Jace. You've hurt me too many times...I..."

"Does this hurt?" Jace pulled her to him and holding her face he planted a passionate kiss on her lips."

Yanking herself free, she hissed loudly, "Stop it you idiot. You're making a spectacle of us. I know why you're doing this – you're claiming me as your property but it's not going to work this time. We're finished." She turned to go.

"Hold on Baby..." Jace grabbed her arm firmly.

"Let me go!" Jorie said, angrily yanking her arm out of his grasp. Hella was just walking back with their drinks. Quickly assessing the situation, she conveniently tripped and the two drinks splashed all over the front of Jace's suit.

"Oopsie," she said, trying to hide a malicious smirk.

"What the hell?" he yelled, looking down at his wet pants and managing to draw the attention of the guests closest to them. Some of them sniggered. His face turned beet red as he stomped off towards the men's room.

"Let's get out of here Hella." Tears were beginning to spill over and she would be completely undone if people noticed. They had already garnered far too much attention. Worst of all, David had witnessed the whole episode.

Outside, waiting for a taxi to come, Jorie said, "I am so damn fed up with men. I think that pervert, Candy, was going to rape me if you hadn't interrupted. And Jace..."

"Ha! That's a laugh! He'd be lucky if he could get it up. Candy is such a disgusting letch, Ickh – He tried it on me last year and Anne-Marie the year before so I figured you were in for a repeat performance. What a phony he is, pretending that he's such a distinguished churchgoer and an upright citizen."

"But why am I a magnet for every sicko and deviant around. You'd think I gave off an 'eau d'pervert' scent," she said, sniffling and laughing.

"C'mon JorJor…it's your god-given attributes. You're boobalicious, the long tawny hair, big brown Bambi eyes, an innocent baby face – a perfect formula for attracting the schmucks of the world. Where is that car?" She began snapping her fingers. It was a habit she had when she was agitated.

"Do you really think he won't tell Mr. Abbott? I hit him pretty hard."

"Good! Tell what? That he tried to rape you? 'Ah' don't think so," she said with a sneer. "Men, they're all a bunch of assholes. Think they can just take whatever they want."

Hella had a hard edge to her, but that was something that drew Jorie to her. She wasn't afraid to say what was on her mind, you knew where you stood with her and you couldn't ask for a more loyal or better friend. Jorie could only think her hardness was a cover-up for a poisonously painful wound - something that had transpired between her and her step-father. Often after several drinks, she would say she hated her step-father with a passion and curse him out, but she wasn't ready to go further. Jorie could only imagine it must have been really ugly because they had no secrets between them.

Chapter Six

Jorie had met Mitch the year before when he came to Montreal from New York to launch his latest book. He was an acquaintance of Vicky's brother and against Jorie's better wishes, Vicky had dragged her along to his reading. *How much more boring can something be than hearing an author drone on and on about a book he wrote.* Vicky insisted they sit right in the front row where Jorie couldn't escape.

When the man himself walked into the room from the side door, Jorie perked up. As soon as he took the podium and introduced himself he had the audience, filled with mostly women, hanging on his every word.

His rumpled, casual wealthy look gave him an air of confidence and for someone nearing mid-life he appeared to be in very good shape – his jacket fitted snuggly over well muscled arms. A tousled chocolate brown mop of unkempt hair badly in need of a styling gave him a boyish looking charm and Jorie had found his startling blue eyes rimmed with black eyelashes mesmerizing. He came into town a couple of times a year and the last time during a break-up with Jace, she had agreed to go on a date with him.

It was January – a freezing cold evening. They had gotten drunk at a downtown bar – Jorie was beginning to think Mitch had a bit of a drinking problem. Afterward in the car, still feeling no pain, he turned the heater on full blast and put the top down, laughing as the vinyl cracked on his rented convertible and thought it was hilarious as they drove onto a wide sidewalk causing the doorman of a ritzy hotel to jump out of the way.

Now, here she was, months later, sitting in the audience listening to him talk about his latest tome. There was no doubt he was a brilliant author and speaker, which probably accounted for his overabundance of confidence. After the talk, and the fans began to dissipate with autographed books tucked under their arms, he came over to Vicky and Jorie. Removing his reading glasses, he placed them in his jacket pocket before taking Jorie's hand and bringing it to his lips. She felt the heat of a blush rise to her face. There was something so chivalrous and sophisticated about him.

"Jorie," he said, taking her other hand in his warm ones, "so glad you could come. I was afraid when we spoke on the phone you might have changed your mind."

She was gratified to see he hadn't been too over-confident about her. He oozed charm and it wouldn't have been hard to fall for him had he not lived in a different city. She also had a niggling feeling that he might be married. He was very adept at avoiding questions he felt would only dampen an otherwise enjoyable occasion.

"Girls, I have a friend in from New York and wonder if you two would like to accompany us for a few drinks not far from here?"

From the back of the room he motioned his friend Rob to join them. They shook hands while Rob and Vicky sized each other up. He was nice looking in a frat boy sort of way with his shirt collar over the neck of his sweater and corduroy pants. A spray of freckles crossed his nose, thick reddish blonde hair was neatly cropped and Vicky was already showing interest in getting to know him better.

They drove across town in Mitch's rented Mercedes to a hotel with a cozy wine cellar in the basement; right off Mitch ordered two bottles of wine. Rob and Vicky seemed to be getting along famously and laughter and conversation flowed as easily as the wine disappeared down their throats. After sharing the second bottle, Jorie knew she was plain drunk. Excusing herself to go to the ladies room her head was swimming and she wished she would have paced herself – she didn't like people seeing this side of her, sloppy drunk.

Almost tipping over as she stood up from the table, Mitch put out a hand to steady her and asked if she wanted help finding the ladies' room; giggling she refused, determined not to appear drunk. Tripping down the hallway she was vaguely aware of the looks she was getting from the hotel guests passing by. Finding the restroom door, she pushed it open and entered one of the cubicles. Plunking down on the toilet seat gratefully, aware that she was weaving, she tried to orientate herself out of the brain fog. It was peaceful in the bathroom and she might have dozed off for a few minutes when she heard a familiar voice. Mitch's voice. He was talking to his friend Rob.

"I don't know where she disappeared to. She was pretty loaded…I should have gone with her – I'll have to ask the hotel staff…"

Quickly climbing onto the toilet seat, she stood up and poked her head over the cubicle top. "Psst, Mish." Heads jerked up from the three men facing the wall of urinals as zippers were quickly yanked up.

"I'm here," she said with a wobbly smile.

Mitch went into gales of laughter as Jorie grinned sheepishly.

The bathroom cleared out as Mitch helped her down off the toilet seat and escorted her back to their table in the wine cellar.

"That's what I like about you Mish. You don't get angry with me."

"That's probably because we don't see each other that often. Let's go back to my hotel and see how we can possibly change that."

Back in the car, Mitch turned the heater on letting the car warm up and he and Jorie began making out in the front seat. Suddenly there was a yelp from behind them, followed by cursing. "She cut me, goddam it! She broke the wine glass she stole and cut me!"

"I wouldn't have cut you if you kept your hands to yourself, you pig!"

"See if there's some tissue in the dash box, Jorie. How bad is it? Do you need to go to the hospital?"

"No," Rob grumbled as Jorie leaned over the front seat, wadded some tissue and began blotting the wound. She wrapped Mitch's clean handkerchief around Rob's bleeding hand, tucking the corner under. Vicky positioned herself as far away as possible in the tight back seat.

"Jesus Christ Rob, I told you they weren't those type of girls."

The fresh air started to sober Jorie up and on the silent drive back to her house, she knew she had to make some changes in her life. And she was glad they didn't end up going back to his hotel. She was beginning to suspect Mitch was married. *And even if he isn't, maybe it's time to tone myself down.*

Chapter Seven

"Mazeltov! You may kiss your bride." David leaned forward and planted a chaste kiss on Devora's cheek. He managed a trite smile to the small gathering of family and friends. The men were pumping his hand. The women watching from the kitchen. His body felt cold and unreal, his insides were vibrating from anxiety. *What have I done? This is my life now?* He looked around at all the satisfied smiling faces – satisfied that they had finally wrapped him up into one of their tidy cocoons. He was having a panic attack. Walls were closing in on him. He became acutely conscious of his drumming heart. Suffocating. Carrying on like everything was normal while inside he thought he was having a heart attack. Why did he go along with his family? Two families decided he and Devora should marry. Did he not have any will of his own? *I hardly know this woman who's standing here beaming from ear to ear. Married for life? What about my own life? Now I'm living for them! All of them that prefer to have their lives laid out for them, tidily sewn up. No decisions – no coloring outside the lines. Stay in your box and behave like the rest of us.*

Married and they had never had more than a passing conversation. Afterwards when they were alone, sitting across from each other at the arborite table in the stark white walled kitchen of the apartment her father had let them have, one of many in his buildings, David found it impossible to talk. *'She's very frum, very religious. Love will come,' the rabbi told me.*

He could not consummate the marriage. He was too embarrassed to be having sex with a strange woman. Oh, he knew of her from his sister Ruth – all the rudimentary facts; she was religious, would make a good wife and came from a good family. What else could he want? *Emotional intimacy.* David didn't think he was a complicated person. His needs were simple. He had been brought up above all, to practice restraint in every facet of his life because there are always consequences to every action. Well that certainly turned out to be true.

***

It was nearing the end of the day when Jorie dropped the files onto David's desk. His back was to her as he stood staring out the window at the dime size drops of rain pelting the glass. Turning, he went to put his hand in his pocket but Jorie noticed the ring first.

"Please tell me that isn't a wedding band," she said incredulously.

"Yes. I was married last week."

"Married? Married!?" she yelped in disbelief, pulling in her chin, her eyebrows raised. "How come you didn't say anything? You know, like mention a girlfriend, an engagement or some little trivial thing like that?"

Shrugging, he said, "what is there to say. I'm married and that's it," he pulled out his chair and sat down reaching over for the stack of folders."

"Oh crap on you Mr. Mystery Man." Jorie felt seriously injured. Beyond angry, she turned on her heel to leave when David called her back.

"Jorie, wait. Come back. Look, I know it's a bit of a surprise, well, a shock maybe, but it's been in the works for a long time. I told you you wouldn't understand my world. She and…"

"She? Does this *she* have a name?"

"Devora. Devora's family and my family are from the old country and have a long history together. Her family was instrumental in saving my parent's lives when they had to flee. It was always understood that we would be married one day. And last week was the day."

"I don't understand. They tell you to marry her and you just do it?"

"I know it seems strange to you, but that's the way our families are."

"But you knew you were going to marry her even when we – I thought there might be something between us. You were just playing me? Do you even love her?" Jorie pulled in her chin again. She was feeling puzzled and incredibly hurt that he hadn't at least mentioned this momentous happening to her so she could have prepared herself. And more than that, she mistakenly thought that slowly they were forming a connection. "What about love? Do you...love her?" She almost choked on the question, afraid of the answer.

"Love? Love is just a simplistic word. It's a catch-word overused in books and ads about romance when what they really mean is lust." A thought crossed his mind that he had no lust for Devora...it might have made their first night together easier if he had. "Real life is not about instant love...it's working together to build a family and love comes eventually."

"Yeah, well I don't know who brain washed you with that bit of drivel, but if that's what you want to believe, then believe it. I think you're just babbling stupid!"

She was so angry! David laughed weakly as she turned and exited his office in a huff. Her words ringing in his ears. And now it was time to go back to the apartment and face Devora. He picked up the stack of folders to work on at home. It was a good shield.

***

It took Jorie time to work through her anger. Things continued as normal at the office. They spoke only when necessary. He knew she was hurt, but it wasn't any of her business and besides, he was the one paying for it. *How can my personal life be such a shit-show and yet my work life be so satisfying.* Mr. Abbott had become like a mentor to him, had given him a generous raise and told him how pleased he was with his work as controller.

One evening, he and Jorie found themselves alone in the office working late. Some of the bitterness Jorie had experienced at first had worn off. She realized that she had conjured up something between her and David that really wasn't there. Every now and then she still felt a sting, but it was a fait accompli and he had made his choice.

"David," she hollered from her office, "I ordered a veg pizza? Want to share?"

The aroma wafted down the hall and David yelled back, "yes!"

Jorie opened a bottle of Mr. Abbott's good red wine in the kitchen and carried a tray with glasses, plates and the pizza box to David's office. There hadn't been much communication between them since he married. She had stopped nursing her hurt feelings and just wanted an easy relationship between them.

Filling the wine glasses she said, "I know it's not kosher wine. You don't have to drink it if you don't want."

David picked up the glass and took a sip. Dry. Not sweet like the syrupy Manischewitz he was used to. He liked it. The pizza was hardly touched by the time they finished the bottle. David, most of it.

Reclining back in his chair holding his wine glass, he said, "I'm getting a divorce."

Jorie jumped. "A divorce? You just got married! It's only been three months!"

His stomach clenched. "The whole community thinks it's my fault."

"Is it?"

"Maybe, partly. As I told you, my family knew her family from way back. It's very hard to keep things hidden in the community I live in. There's not many secrets. Or maybe I should say, there are many secrets, just not many well hidden. But somehow Devora managed. I can't tell them she was having an affair with the rabbi of a congregation across town. Her reputation would be ruined."

Jorie's eyes widened, she pulled in her chin and sat back. "An affair? But, but, you're newlyweds." She had noticed David seemed to be exhibiting a lot of inner turmoil these last few weeks. Now she understood.

"I think you're confusing your version of newlyweds with the secular viewpoint. Devora was not any happier with our marriage than I was it turns out. Apparently she had been seeing and studying the Torah with a conservative rabbi across town before we married – I don't think her parents were aware – they would not have approved…after we married, she said she went to him to talk about the problems we were having and one thing led to another."

"How did you find out?"

"We had a heated argument and I told her I didn't think I could continue with the marriage – she was furious and spit out it was my fault she was having an affair. She said she loves him and he was fulfilling her spiritual as well as physical needs and that he shares her interests in mysticism. And, of course, he flattered her by saying she had very high ideals and needed somebody special to understand her."

"Well that sounds like a load of…Wow! – So are you separating or…?"

"We're still living together, unpleasant as it is, because you have no idea of the scandal this is going to cause. Not only for my family, but the Rabbi's – he's married with kids – and, and, it's a mess," he said, pinching the bridge of his nose. He had repressed everything so tightly that it was both frightening to hear himself say it out loud and a release of intense pressure that had been building up – as if he had lanced a great boil letting the nasty contents spill out. The wine had obviously loosened his tongue.

"It's not like it's never happened before David. You're not the first person to get a divorce."

"You don't understand the religious community. You never can. If you weren't brought up like that…It's very close-knit…there are reasons, you know." David lowered his eyes. He felt a lump in the pit of his stomach. "We have to stick together – my parents aren't like yours. They went through hell to give us a life here and those are bonds that are hard to go against. You know, when my mother lived in Poland, some Russian soldiers came to her house. She was only sixteen – they said they needed a girl to work in the barracks kitchen. Her mother, my grandmother, who I never knew, said, 'take her'. She was one of five sisters. She used to risk her life sneaking potato and carrot peelings to bring home so the family wouldn't starve. And whatever else happened, she never talks about it. My mother is a very strong person."

Jorie found herself fascinated and profoundly moved. She poured him another glass of wine. "Come, let's sit on the sofa in the waiting area. We'll be more comfortable."

Taking his hand, she led him towards the entrance.

Seating herself in an armchair, David sat down on the sofa. Jorie then felt the gap between them too wide to have such an intimacy revealed and moved over to the sofa. "David, can you tell me a bit about your childhood? How you were brought up. You might find we have more similarities than not."

A cynical laugh burst from him. "Similarities? Not a chance. I told you, you haven't got a clue."

"Well, try me. I'd really like to know."

Chapter Eight

1952 January – 12 years earlier

Ow, ow, ow! A thousand needles pricked his skin. The fluffy white snowflakes had transformed into tiny freezing projectiles biting his cheeks and stinging his nose. Using his tongue he pushed the soggy bits of wool scarf from his mouth just as he stumbled over a snowbank spilling his books onto the street. He had trouble gathering them up his fingers were so brittle, but he managed to grasp the siddur just as it was in danger of being run over. Kissing it, he stuffed it into his bag.

Only a few more steps to the front door. His empty stomach growled in anticipation of the hot soup his mother would have waiting for him…rich, unhatched chicken eggs nesting under the broad yellow noodles – he could already taste it. Ruth always whined that he got extra, and secretly David knew it was because he was his mother's favorite. He smiled inwardly as saliva pooled in his mouth and dribbled onto the wet fusty scarf.

The three story red brick tenement building on Clark Street had an austere, worn façade. Wooden balconies hung precariously over the sidewalk. David stood on the stoop reaching up to touch the mezuza with his frozen fingers and then struggled to fit the key into the keyhole. Flinging open the door he was hit with a blast of heat and he breathed a sigh of relief as the warm air engulfed him.

Yanking the sodden scarf from his face he caught the rivulets of melting ice dripping off his hair with his tongue. Thirty-one, thirty-two, thirty-three he counted as he ran up the wooden stairs to the third floor flat.

Turning the bronze door knob, he stumbled into the tiny kitchen and dropped his bookbag in the corner. Still frozen hands tugged off his damp jacket, the one both his older brother and sister had worn until they outgrew it, and hung it on a peg. Easing his cold bum onto a rickety painted chair he pushed his boots off kicking them over near the gas stove. *Ma is going to be mad when she sees all the water on the floor.* Where was his Ma he suddenly realized. She was usually there to greet him and come to think of it, he didn't see anything cooking on the wood stove. The Pa was gone to the country peddling, Ruth and Adam wouldn't be home till later he knew, but somebody should be here.

"Morty! I told you. Only the bottom drawer is for us!" *Aunt Esther's voice!* His shoulders drooped as he grimaced.

Treading lightly along the squeaky wooden floorboards, he peeked around the corner into the first bedroom. Aunt Esther's suitcase was on the brass bed and she was handing clothing to his twelve-year-old cousin Morty. She spotted him immediately.

"Dovey! Why didn't you tell me you were home? Come in boychick!" she yelled. He tentatively took a step into the room – before he could escape, Esther clutched him to her large soft bosom and planted kisses all over his squashed head.

"Oy! A frozen ponem!" she said, grabbing his cold face in her hands. "Morty, why didn't you tell me your cousin Dovey was home!"

"How could I know Ma? – I was in here with you." David was happy to see Morty, but Aunt Esther was a force to be reckoned with.

"Never mind. Come, come boychick, you must be hungry. I'll make you a hamburger."

"Where's my Ma? I don't like hamburgers."

"Whaat? You're not happy to see me? And your cousin Morty?" Morty turned his hands palms up and cast a look of resignation at David.

"Your mamila's gone to the hospital to bring home a new baby. Isn't that wonderful? Now, come, sit, sit. It's freezing out there. You must be hungry," she pushed him toward the kitchen in front of her. "Such a big boy for only ten years old. Isn't he Morty." Morty shrugged his shoulders. Esther pulled the table away from the wall so both David and Morty could have a place to sit. Turning around to the icebox she took out a prepared hamburger and placed it in a meat frypan.

"I don't like hamburgers," David said, trying to sort out all the new information. He knew his mother was pregnant, but he didn't know she was going to the hospital today or that Aunt Esther was coming.

"Whaaat? What boy doesn't like hamburgers! I make the best. Try it, you'll like it, won't he Morty." Morty rolled his eyes. Taking the thin piece of meat out of the pan, she placed it on the chipped floral meat plate next to a dill pickle and a slice of Challah bread. "You want mustard, ketchup? I'll make you a nice cup of tea."

"I don't like tea."

"You'll like my tea Dovey, won't he Morty. It will warm you up," she said placing the kettle on the stove to boil.

He felt himself getting anxious. Last year his mother had been pregnant and when he came home from school, there was blood all over the stairs.

"Where's Adam?"

"Now don't fuss. Your brother had to go to the dentist after school."

"I'm not fussing," David replied in a barely audible voice. "And my sister?"

"Ruth is staying with her friend Hannah until the storm blows over. Morty, you remember cousin Ruth's friend Hannah? Such a nice young maidila. You should be lucky to get a wife like Hannah one day."

David spread some mustard onto the bread, wrapped it around the pickle and took a bite. With Aunt Esther's back turned to them, Morty pointed at the hamburger signaling he would eat it. David nodded and Morty quickly snatched it cramming it into his mouth.

"A-ha...so I see," Esther said, eyeing the empty plate. "What boy doesn't like hamburgers," she said, whisking the plate into the rusted ironstone sink.

A gust of warmth blew in as the kitchen door opened and Adam came in – his cheeks red and the defrosting ice on his coat dripping off his shoulders.

"Brrr, it's freezing in here." He took off his mitts and hat, beating the snow off on his pants and hung them on the clothes-line over the stove. Water sizzled as it dropped onto the hot burner.

"Here Adam, have some tea," Aunt Esther said, snatching the untouched mug from in front of David and handing it to Adam. "You're hungry?"

"No. I ate after school. Did you hear anything from the hospital?"

"Not yet, not yet boychik. Your Ma will be fine."

The phone rang. Aunt Esther quickly picked it up and said, "Yes? Yes, hello? Malka it's you?

A very disgruntled voice on the other end of the line told her in no uncertain terms that it wasn't Malka and she should stop trying to listen in on her conversations.

Esther hung up the receiver and looked at the kids with a puzzled face.

"That wasn't our ring Auntie. That's Mrs. Bleck's ring – she gets really annoyed if we answer by mistake. We have a party-line with her and another tenant," Adam said.

The next day, the storm had abated and Ruth came home after school. "Ruth! Ruth!" shouted Aunt Esther rushing towards the door, "such a beautiful girl and so tall since I last saw you!" She took Ruth's face in her strong hands and kissed her eight times, three times on each cheek and twice on her forehead. "Oy! A shanya ponem! A real beauty you are. You're hungry? Come children, dinner is served." David caught a smirk from Ruth. Aunt Esther reminded David of the steam rollers he saw in the summer squashing down the new pavement.

"Aunt Esther, I'm fourteen and Adam's fifteen. We're hardly children anymore," Ruth said, her chin defiantly raised as she pulled back her long dark hair and fastened it into a pony tail.

"Yes, yes. You're all grown up," Aunt Esther clucked. "Anyway, dinner is served Madame. Please take your seat."

Esther ladled out the stewed chicken along with a piece of carrot and a boiled potato onto each plate. The four kids shared a look and quickly began exchanging food with each other.

Aunt Esther, with hands on her broad hips, exclaimed, "whaat is this?"

"I like dark meat and Ruth only likes the white and no potatoes and Adam doesn't like carrots," David said, scraping a piece of meat off his stringy chicken leg.

"You should be more like my Morty. He's a good boy. He eats everything, don't you Morty?" Morty caught unawares glanced up and garbled. "Yes Ma," his mouth full of hot potato.

Ruth piped up. "David's so skinny, the Pa pays him to eat. He calls him a bag of bones."

David's face reddened.

"Ruth." Adam flashed her a warning look. "Enough."

***

"Here, let me help you Malka. It's too soon for you to be walking so much. Oy! Forty-six and still having babies," Esther said, taking the baby from her arms and moving the blanket away from her face, fussing over her.

"Morty, pick up the valise. Do I have to tell you!" Malka was winded by the time she reached the third floor. It had been a long trek home from the hospital with the baby in one arm and the suitcase in the other, especially difficult climbing over the snowbanks.

"I think Zev could have made more of an effort to get home with the car," Esther huffed under her breath. When they were younger, Esther had liked Zev. But after the never to be spoken about incident, he became more religious, he stopped being the easy-going man she first knew and gradually became more reclusive with a definite edge to his personality. Last time she had visited, he even went to sleep in the 'shvitz' rather than be sociable. Imagine, sleeping at the Colonial Baths so he wouldn't have to visit, she, hmphed to herself.

Malka didn't want to argue. She was bone-tired and just wanted to lie down and sleep. "Esther, the snow storm. To drive forty miles in a blizzard is dangerous. Better he should stay there. How were the children?"

"Oh, no problem, no problem, children are children."

What does that mean Malka thought wearily. The buzzer rang. Morty ran to the curtained window looking down at the street.

"It's the iceman!"

"Oy," Malka sighed. "Ice we have plenty of outdoors and yet still we have to pay for it. There's money in the jar on the first shelf."

"Morty! Pull the cord to let him in." Esther yelled.

The iceman grunted as he trudged up the three flights of stairs tightly gripping the tongs holding the block of ice.

"Come in, come in Mister. Right over there. Oh, you've been here before so you know," Esther said, trying to get out of his way in the tiny kitchen. "Don't worry about the sawdust. I'll clean it up. Tsk tsk. Morty, get the broom."

Just as the iceman left, David came in the kitchen door looking completely disheveled.

"Vas is dis?" Aunt Esther grabbed his face turning it this way and that, not realizing that it hurt like hell. "What happened Dovey? Who did this?"

"Nothing... I, I tripped and fell, that's all."

"Oohh, my my. That must have been a very bad fall," she said, closely scrutinizing his face and clothes through narrowed eyes. "Well, good news. Your Mamala is home with a new baby sister, but before you go to see her I'm going to clean you up. You don't want she should have a heart attack on top of everything." She grabbed a rag off the sink running it under the cold water tap and began scrubbing his cut face.

"Ow! You're hurting me!"

"And this schmata – what is this?" she said pulling at the torn pocket and sleeve. "Tsk, tsk. Give to me the jacket and go see your Ma and new baby sister."

David felt calmer now that his mother was safely at home.

Later that evening, in the bedroom he shared with Adam and now Morty, Morty, taking in David's purplish yellow eye with undisguised admiration, asked David what happened.

"I was on my way home from the Yeshiva. My belt buckle broke and my pants kept falling down. I had to keep holding them up with one hand and my books in the other. Some 'nice' boys from St. Michael's came along – called me a Yid. They tried to pull my tzitzis. I forgot to take off my yarmulke and they beat me up. That's all."

"Did ya get in a couple of good licks at least?"

"How could I? I just told you, I was holding up my pants. If I would have dropped my books, they would have kicked them into the snow. They cost money, you know. Luckily some people came along and they ran off. Sometimes, when I'm by myself, I take off my keepa and put it in my pocket," David said, sinking onto the bed and examining his belt and the broken buckle.

"Don't you feel guilty when you hide it?"

"It's better than getting beaten up," he said, as he laid aside the unfixable buckle. *I'll have to borrow a belt from Adam tomorrow, but Ruth's would probably fit me better. I know she won't lend hers though.*

"In New York where we live there are lots of Yidden and I'm not afraid," Morty said, lowering his eyes to the floor.

"How long are you and Auntie staying?"

"I heard her tell your Ma she would stay as long as she needs her."

David pursed his mouth to the side and scowled. He liked his cousin Morty well enough. Being almost the same age he was easy to be friends with. But he definitely didn't like Aunt Esther's cooking. And she was bossy. And always hugging and kissing him. With Esther out of earshot, David said to Morty, "let's ask if we can go out on the street after we finish eating. Do you think she'll let us?"

Ruth walking by the room overheard and piped up. "You know the Pa wouldn't like it. You're supposed to study."

"Yeah, but the Pa's not here and Ma won't mind. And why do you always have to butt in miss buttinsky buttnick? Okay, Morty? You ask her," David said.

"Yes, yes. Go." Esther said, wiping her hands on her apron and replacing the plates on the open shelf. "The fresh air will help you sleep. But only for an hour, understand? You have homework."

It was dark on the street but David headed through a tight space between the buildings that led into the back lane. The only lights were the ones from inside the windows reflecting on the snow.

"Morty...want to see something?"

"What?"

"You'll see. Follow me."

They walked along the ruts of snow left behind by the snowplow. A few buildings farther down David said, "here, come," he motioned with his hand, finger to his lips, and crouched down in a small corner between two chimneys.

"What is it?" Morty's eyes were wide with anticipation as he squeezed in beside David.

"Look." David pointed to a window almost at eye level. Inside the light was on and a woman was breastfeeding her baby in a rocking chair. They watched for a few minutes until the woman detached the child and got up to lay him in his cradle leaving her breast uncovered.

Morty gasped. "Did you see that! I saw her – "

Voices coming along the lane made them jump. David grabbed Morty's sleeve and they both ran slipping and sliding down the lane giggling and laughing.

***

"Esther, a gitten dank, thank you so much," Malka said, giving Esther a warm hug.

"Anytime Malkala…oh, I see our taxi down below. Morty. Schlep the suitcase. Do I have to tell you? Good-bye my love. Write to me." Esther grabbed Malka's face and kissed her all over.

Chapter Nine

The bubble of intimacy burst when the door from the hallway opened and the janitor entered pushing his wagon before him, surprised to see two people sitting there.

Jorie had been so mesmerized by David's story she was startled and annoyed. She didn't want this tiny bit of closeness to end.

"Well, that was a marathon speech. It's not really my nature", he said glancing at the empty wine bottle and then his watch. "We better get out of here and let him do his job or we'll find ourselves locked in."

That wouldn't be so bad, Jorie thought. "David, thanks for sharing with me. You had such a rich childhood."

"Rich?" David said, helping Jorie into her coat.

"You know, interesting people…"

"I guess I'm still not far enough away to see it like that. C'mon, I'll give you a lift home."

***

A few days later…

"Jorie, we're going to the club after work tonight. Want to come with?"

"Thanks Vicky, but I'll pass. I have something to do this evening." She didn't want to tell her that she and David were having dinner together. It wasn't a date, just friends getting together and she didn't want any talk spreading in the office.

***

After a dinner of Greek salad and glazed grilled salmon along with a couple of glasses of wine, Jorie encouraged David to pick up his story where it had ended.

"How old were you at the time?"

"I was probably around ten years old."

1952 – Summer

"David, the Pa will be home tomorrow morning. We have to get ready for Shabbos. Fetch me the chicken out of the bathtub so I can take it to the schochet." His mother's voice was always low and soft – never commanding. The day before he and his mother had gone to the Rachel St. farmer's market and bought the chicken. David giggled as his mother blew the feather's apart on the chicken's pipek to see if it was fresh.

"Ma, I'm afraid of the chicken. The last one tried to peck my eyes out. Can't Adam do it?"

"Adam is busy. Now be a brave boy. Here's a bag."

"Can we stop at the shoe store so I can see my skeleton in the x-ray machine?"

"Not today. We have to go to the Kosher bakery to get a challah before they run out."

"Ma? What would happen if we ate bread from the POM bakery instead of from the Kosher bakery? The air always smells so good when they're baking."

"It's not for us."

"But why isn't it for us? It's just bread isn't it?"

"David, don't talk like that. You know it makes the Pa angry when you start this."

"Okay Ma. But…"

"No David, it's not for us."

"Well, can we go to Zlotis and buy an ice cream?"

"Not today. I don't have extra money. If the Pa had a good week, maybe next time we'll be able."

David twisted his mouth. "Alllright." He wasn't really angry. He knew if his mother had the extra money, she never refused him anything.

He was glad the Pa would be coming home. At night with his bedroom door cracked open he could see his father in the dim light working on his books at the kitchen table – it made him feel safe as he climbed back into bed and drifted off to sleep.

***

David, his nose pressed against the window, saw the police car pull up to the curb. Down below, his friends on the street excitedly dropped their hockey sticks and gathered around the car. More than anything he wanted to be outside with them, but his father's harsh words reverberated in his mind, 'you want to be a laidigaier, a loafer, a bum all your life? Study is what's important – play, play, anybody can play, what does that do for you.'

The buzzer rang. Through the thin walls he heard heavy boots clomping up the stairs to the third floor. *Why would the police be coming here?* His heart raced in his chest. *Storm troopers!* Uncle Levi's stories about escaping from Russia came vividly to mind. The Pa never talked about his life in Russia, but Uncle Levi filled David's head with thrilling, frightening stories about their life 'over there'. You couldn't have a nightmare as scary as some of Uncle Levi's stories, David thought.

Jumping up, he ran down the hall to the kitchen, "Ma! Ma! Don't open the door! It's the police!"

"Hush Dovey," she said in Yiddish, wiping her hands on her apron.

"But maybe they're going to take the Pa away!" he cried, stepping behind her as she opened the door.

"Sirs, yes?" His mother, being illiterate, had never mastered English and at best spoke a bastardized version of Yiddish and English.

Adam came from the back room shouldering his way to the front of the narrow kitchen entrance. Ruth was his father's favorite and Adam was the prince of the family. He had a certain kind of bravado and confidence for a fifteen-year-old that David both admired and envied about his older brother.

"Is Mr. Kaisman at home?" the police officer asked.

Adam spoke up. "No sir. He's away in the country."

"Well young man, perhaps you can give him a message for us. The gangster your dad beat up several years ago when he tried to rob your father's pawn shop is being released from prison and we thought we should give your dad a warning. It might be a good idea to take precautions." The officer nodded and tipped his hat toward Malka.

Adam turned, translating the message to his mother in Yiddish. Color rose in her cheeks, but she thanked the police and shut the door.

"Adam, run downstairs and tell your uncle."

"I'm coming with," David said, running out the door on Adam's heels.

Skipping briskly down the stairs they passed the landing of the second floor units. One of the doors was open to let the heat in from the stairway. Faigie Finkelstein's father was sitting on the sofa watching wrestling on his black and white TV. His leg flew up with a grunt and a yelp as his right arm shot into the air. He was kicking and punching as if he himself were the wrestler. David and Adam looked at each other covering their mouths to muffle their laughter. As they continued on down to the ground floor they passed Chickie, the taxi driver, just coming home from work. He gave them a gruff hello as they banged on the uncle's door. A pungent, peppery scent of oranges lingered in the hallway and tickled their nostrils. They knew Mrs. Bleck in unit 2A was at home. They never saw her without a bag of oranges in her hand. Sometimes when she left her door open, they would see her sitting on her bed with orange peels all over the blanket.

Cracking open the door of 1A, a tiny wizened woman with a bandana tightly wrapped around her forehead peeked out. Their mother had told them that Auntie always wore the bandana because she suffered from terrible headaches and found the tight pressure helped to ease them.

"Auntie Brunya, is uncle Levi here?" Adam asked.

Motioning them in, they stepped up as their feet sank into squashy layered Persian carpets. It was like walking on sponges.

Uncle Levi was a peddler and their father used to sneer and say that Levi kept more junk than he ever sold. David always had the feeling his father resented Uncle Levi – he couldn't quite figure out why, but he had the feeling some of it was from jealousy.

The flat gave off a musty, antiquey smell. Lining the left wall were a dozen grandfather clocks, not one of them set at the correct time which had them chiming at all hours of the day. Assorted cuckoo clocks framed a window on the wall above the sofa on the right. A fat calico cat perched precariously on the back of the sofa in anticipation of a cuckoo popping out. Two gray kittens wrestled with a sock shaped into a ball on the soft carpets. Their auntie and uncle had a tender spot for stray cats and many were invited in when the nights turned cold.

"We need to see Uncle Levi," David said breathlessly, tugging on the neck of his shirt and dancing from one foot to the other.

"Come," her gnarled fingers grasping her cane, she pointed to the end of the room directing them.

Following her down a dimly lit hallway they navigated through a maze of dark heavy furniture covered with unopened boxes and 'chatchcas' of every sort. Uncle Levi was working at his desk in the back room and swiveled the chair around to face them.

"Boys, how nice to see you. Vat can I help you vith today. You don't come often to see your old uncle. Must be important." A little black panther lay on top of the desk on a pile of papers, languidly wagging his tail, he gazed at them through narrowed yellow eyes.

Adam quickly told him about the police warning. The uncle listened and for a long time sat there quietly nodding his head up and down, his tired eyes glazed, as if he were somewhere far away.

"So, that's not good. But don't you boys vurry. It vill be fine. I'll talk wit your fadder when he comes back. Come here my little Dovey," he said reaching out with his legs and scissoring David between them. "Vat a big boy – how old are you now? Must be at least ready for Bar Mitzvah?"

David giggled. "No, Uncle, I'm still only ten."

"Only ten and already so tall and handsome." Uncle Levi started singing a song – a happy holiday song, "Yismechu bemalchutch…" wiggling David back and forth. Uncle Levi had no children of his own and David liked being his favorite because often he would give him a quarter or a couple of times even a dollar and some candy along with a short lecture. "You save your money. You're going to go to school and be important. Not a peddler like me, farshtaist? You understand?" Not loosening his grip on the dollar bill until David promised him he would. Whenever he got a dollar, he always gave it to his mother, but change he kept for himself in a small box hidden in the corner of his drawer in the dresser he shared with Adam.

Once in a while he would take the precious money box out, go into the bathroom, the only room with a lock, and stack all the money in little piles. Dimes on top of dimes, nickels on top of nickels and the best, quarters. He had almost $9.15 saved up, which he knew was a great deal of money. Unfolding the worn page from the Sears catalog he looked with yearning at the new Schwinn Phantom with the torpedo headlight, $54.95, a king's amount of money. The week before he had the change all laid out on the arborite surrounding the sink when his father banged on the door. Unnerved, he tried to scoop up the change and dropped two whole quarters into the toilet at the same time he flushed and watched in dismay as they went down the drain. His face puckered up and he wanted to cry, but what good would that do. It took him a long time to stop berating himself for his clumsiness.

Uncle Levi released his hold on David, reached into his left pocket and handed the boys wrapped humbugs. And from his other pocket gave them two quarters each.

"Now run upstairs like good boys and tell your Ma not to vurry. I vill talk to your fadder when he comes home." They both shouted over their shoulders, "thank you uncle Levi," as they turned and ran down the hall stepping up onto the spongy carpets in the living room, Auntie Brunya called after them… "you're hungry? You like some honey cake? Very fresh."

"No thank you Auntie – we have to tell Ma what uncle Levi said." Breathlessly they raced back up the stairs.

Bursting into the kitchen, Adam repeated what Levi had told them and showed his mother the two quarters. "Very nice. Put one in the Pishka box and save the other." David glared at Adam. *Why did he have to tell her?* The Pishka box was for the poor. Weren't they just as poor? All his friends had bicycles except him.

Two nights later, the Pa came home from the country. David, Ruth and Adam listened with big ears as his mother and father discussed the probability of the gang of thugs finding them and creating trouble. David knew his father had beaten the thief badly and the crook had been left with permanent damage. His father was strong and coming from Russia, that was the way crooks were dealt with. The punk had cost Zev his pawn shop business when his gang had come back and smashed the windows and tried to set it on fire. He had made a good living for the family then. Now he was forced to drive to the country and peddle to the farmers. He used a different name, Monsieur Jean, to disguise being Jewish. Adam had told David that one time when he went with his father a man drove by and the farmer pointed and said, 'that guy is a Jew.'

***

David was lying in bed trying to rouse himself from a deep sleep. School had ended for the summer, bringing a contented half-smile to his lips. He luxuriated in the thought of almost two whole months without classes. But still, his father would want him to study over the summer. "Kum, learnen." Whenever his father was home, it was the same thing. "Come, study, learn."

Would there ever be a time when he wouldn't have to hear those words? All winter he envied his friends playing on the hockey teams, the Peretz Shul Peewees against the Talmud Torah Tornados. If his father was out of town, after school he would strap a couple of thick catalogs around his legs and volunteer to be goalie. He had painted Ruth's skates black. Adam's skates, bought second hand, were in too bad shape to be useable. You could still tell they were girl's skates by the points on the toes, but it was better than nothing.

Through the gauzy curtain, the bright morning sunlight played over his eyes. He turned onto his side snuggling the thin flannel blanket about him and noticed Adam's bed was empty. At the same time he heard pounding and loud voices coming from the kitchen. Throwing the cover off, he jumped out of bed in his T-shirt and pajama bottoms and crept down the hallway unsure of what to expect. Peeking around the corner into the kitchen he saw his father pounding and pounding the wooden table with his big fist. Dishes and cups on the table were jumping. David trembled. What was wrong with the Pa? Suddenly Zev stopped pounding and his head fell to his arms. His father's back was shaking. He was crying! Adam and his mother were standing there frozen and Uncle Levi was talking quietly to Zev, his hand on his brother's shaking shoulder. David tugged on the neck of his shirt – it was the most frightening thing he could ever imagine.

Adam spotted David and came to him in the hallway.

"What happened? What's wrong with the Pa?" David whispered swallowing hard.

Adam took a deep breath. David could see his brother's face was paler than usual and Adam was shaking, which scared him even more. Adam was always the calm, reasonable one. Whatever happened must be very bad. David kept tugging on the neck of his shirt.

"The Pa was supposed to leave for the country but when he went downstairs, he found his tires slashed, the car broken into and all the merchandise he was going to peddle, stolen. He's crying that he can't get a break. That everything he does turns to shit."

"Holy cow!" David whispered, his heart racing a mile-a-minute. He knew it was a momentous thing that had happened. Just the day before he had heard his mother discussing with the neighbor lady how bad things were and how much she prayed that Zev would have a good week. Early in the season, the farmers didn't have much money left from the winter and they couldn't pay the running tabs they owed from January until they started to earn from their crops.

David and Adam sat in their room staring at each other. Ruth joined them with tears running down her cheeks. They didn't know what to do to help their father.

After a while they heard Uncle Levi leave and the Pa called the boys and Ruth into the kitchen. They stood facing him, nervously staring with big eyes not daring to think what he was going to say. Maybe he's going to leave us, David thought, tugging on the neck of his tee-shirt.

"I need some money to replace the tires," he said, his voice low and wooden. His eyes were bloodshot and he looked suddenly very old. "Without the tires, I can't go to the country. Do you have any money to contribute?" David could see what a toll it was taking on the Pa to ask his children for money, but he wanted a bike like all the other kids. He really wanted it!

Adam came back from his room with $28.00 he had saved from delivering groceries. Ruth contributed $14.00 from babysitting and David gave $2.00. It was an agonizing decision – he took his money box from the back of the dresser and locked himself in the bathroom. First he counted out five dollars, but then he would only have $4.15 left – that was a long way from the $54.95 he needed for the bike. So he decided that he would give all the quarters to his father and keep only the small change. But even then, he sighed, it was still over half his savings. Ultimately he decided that $2.00 was all he could spare. That left him with $7.15 to put towards the bike. He felt ashamed of himself and angry that he would never, ever have enough to buy a bicycle before he was too old to ride it! Fear and frustration were building up inside him. He took the $2.00 and laid it on the table with the other money, avoiding his father's eyes. He let himself out of the kitchen door and ran down the stairs in a frenzy onto the street.

Seeing his friend Hymie's bike lying on the sidewalk, overcome with rage, he jumped up and down until the spokes were busted and the front wheel bent. Hymie, who was a year older and almost a head taller, came running from out of nowhere and punched David in the shoulder. David landed hard on the pavement, but rebounded and recovering from the blow, managed to connect a closed fist with Hymie's eye and then Hymie let him have it but good. It was a relief to let out the tension of his anger even if he got the worst of it.

After dinner, Malka was ironing a pair of Zev's pants on the kitchen table when there was a banging on the kitchen door. David was sitting on the floor by the stove trying to fix a transistor radio he had found in the garbage. Zev opened the door to be confronted with Hymie's father, face like a red pomegranate, eyes bulging. No pleasantries were exchanged – only the sound of a booming voice. "You owe my kid a new bike," Hymie's father bellowed. The whole building could hear him. David knew he was in trouble for sure. He started to shake with fear. There was only the kitchen door and he couldn't make a run for it there, not with the two men roaring at each other, so he quickly exited to the safety of his bedroom.

"That ruffian of yours busted my son's bike to hell and gave him a black eye to boot."

This was all Zev needed to hear. Slamming the kitchen door, David heard his father's heavy footsteps coming towards his room and quickly shut his bedroom door. He stood in the center of the room tugging hard on the neck of his shirt. There was no where to run. Adam who had been studying at his desk stood up, eyes as round as saucers. Holding his hands palms up he looked questioningly at David and mouthed, "what's happened?" The bedroom door crashed open, the doorknob hitting the wall behind as a stone-faced Zev spun his belt from his trouser loops, grabbed David by the arm and began viciously strapping him over and over, taking out all his pent up rage and frustration. David screamed. Zev had him in an iron grip and in a struggle to get loose, the edge of the leather strap hit his bare arm leaving a fiery red mark.

Quickly, Malka put the iron down and ran after Zev. "Stop! Stop!" she cried, grabbing Zev's arm. "It's enough! He's just a little boy!" Adam too tried to hold him back, but Zev was stronger than both of them and threw them off.

Ruth stood there sobbing and pleading. "Pa, Pa stop it! Please!"

Finally, Zev flung his belt viciously onto the floor and stomped out of the room. After it was over, David lay on his stomach sobbing as Malka administered some soothing salve to the raw and bleeding welts. His tears were due less to the pain than to the inherent injustice and humiliation of having no way to defend himself. He loved his father above everything but at this moment he hated him just as fiercely and worried he would have to go through life at the mercy of a tyrant.

Later that evening after things had quieted down, Mr. Nadler the insurance salesman, who lived in the building, had the badly timed idea to stop by unannounced.

"Heard you've had some problems with those blood sucking bandits, Zev," Nadler said, trying to sound genuinely solicitous. Reaching into his briefcase he pulled out assorted company pens and pencils for the children placing them on the kitchen table. Ruth and Adam's eyes lit up. David was still too sore and humiliated to come out of his room but he knew Adam would save him some.

"Now would be a good time to buy some insurance, in case they do anything else."

Zev went ballistic. "Insurance? You think I have money for insurance? Go on, get out of my house you bum!"

"That was terrible!" Jorie exclaimed. She couldn't imagine anyone going through something like that and especially being strapped by your own parent. She wanted to hug David, to hold him and comfort him, but he had related the story so dispassionately that she wasn't sure what reaction he expected of her. "What happened with the tires and the clothing they stole? Was your Dad able to come up with the money?"

"My uncle Levi gave him what he needed from the rent money bank account. Uncle Levi and my father had pooled what little money they had earned when they first came to Canada and used it as a down payment for the building – but Uncle Levi always insisted that all the rent money go into the bank so they could pay the building off and buy another. I think my father always resented Levi because even though he was only a rag picker, you know, he picked up old furniture and junk and peddled it with his horse and wagon, Levi was a good saver and a better businessman. And I really think I've bored you enough for one day."

"David, please, no. It's not boring at all. It's so different from my upbringing, I, I can't even imagine..."

David savored a mouthful of wine while he pondered why he was telling her all this. It went against his very grain to allow himself to be vulnerable and telling her these things out loud, while somewhat cathartic, was also bringing up long buried painful emotions. He had never laid himself bare, even to Adam, who had lived through it with him. Whatever the family problems, they were always neatly packaged up and put away somewhere safely in the dark reaches of the mind never to be discussed in the family again. It was life. That was the way it was and talking about it wouldn't change anything. Although, now that he had started, he felt like he had opened a faucet and there seemed to be no handle to shut it off.

Chapter Ten

1953 December

I remember when I was eleven, I came home from school one winter day and found my mother sobbing at the kitchen table. I froze. Something horrible must have happened. She had had three miscarriages but there was no sign of blood anywhere. Ruth was standing by her side with her arms around her neck.

"Ma, please stop crying, it's not so bad," said Ruth plaintively.

"My knife! My only knife!" Ruth looked at David beseechingly as Malka wiped her eyes with the heels of her hands.

"She found the blade in the ashes when she cleaned out the stove this morning. It must have fallen into the oven and she didn't notice. The handle burned up. It's from the old country and the only thing she had from her mother."

David felt bad but relieved at the same time. His mother was the strongest person he knew. He had never seen her cry before and now to see her sitting there with big tears rolling down her cheeks, he was paralyzed with fear and tugged on the neck of his shirt. Suddenly aware that David was standing there in his winter jacket, snow melting onto the worn wooden floor and his boots soaking wet, his mother wiped her eyes with her apron. Getting up, she pulled a chair over towards the stove.

"Come Dovey," she wrenched open the oven door. "Sit here and put your feet on the door. Dry off. Get warm," she said pulling herself together. Removing his scarf from his neck she pushed him onto the wooden chair in front of the stove.

"The Pa will be home soon; it's Shabbos, I have to start supper." She glanced at the blade in the sink. Choking back sobs, she let out a series of small guttural sounds. David sensed that somehow the loss of this knife had come to symbolize her whole life of hardship and grief.

David was desperate. He loved his mother so much. She was always making sacrifices to buy them things they needed. He knew what he had to do.

The next morning very early, the sun was out reflecting bright and blinding off the snow. Rising before anyone else, he put on his kippah and dressed quietly – it was Shabbos. Taking the money from his hiding place in the drawer, he dropped it into a sock and pocketed the sock securely in his winter jacket. Leaving the house through the kitchen, the aroma of cholent heating through the night made his stomach grumble. He had never gone to a store on Shabbos or even dared to count his money – you weren't allowed to carry anything on Shabbos, but this was an emergency. His father would be more than angry if he got caught, but he could only focus on one thought. Anything to ease his mother's pain from her broken heart.

All the Jewish shops in their neighborhood were closed on Saturday, but he knew the hardware store several blocks away would be open. His friends often talked about 'the others' and their way of living.

Leaving the streets of his neighborhood that were so familiar to him was like entering a different world. A world where life went on even if it was Shabbos. The Goyim's world. Coming to the hardware store he was relieved to see it was already open. He took a deep breath and hesitantly pushed on the door. A bell fastened to the door gave a loud clang and banged against the glass. His heart jumped into his throat at the sound. It made him feel like an intruder or worse, a thief. Glancing around, he saw the shop keeper sitting by the window on a chair. He could feel the man's eyes zeroing in on him as he strolled up and down the aisles. Tugging on the neck of his shirt, he spotted the showcase of knives. It was locked. He swallowed hard. His heart was beating like a drum. Now he would have to ask the shop keeper for the key.

"Can I help you young man?"

David jumped and turning, stared up at the face of the thin man and the man, with his arms behind his back, stared down at him thru wire-rimmed spectacles.

He screwed up all his courage. "I would like to buy a kitchen knife sir. Your best one."

"A knife eh? And what would a boy your age need with a knife?"

"My mother burned hers in the oven and she's very upset. She cried a long time when she found the blade – she never cries. She's very strong."

"I see." A long silence ensued. "Well, how much do you have to spend?" he asked, taking in the kippah and David's pale face. He knew that Jews in his area didn't venture out on Saturdays except to go to Synagogue.

"I have seven dollars and fifteen cents."

Taking the key out of his pocket he unlocked the glass case and selected a sharp looking butcher knife. David's face reddened and he stepped back. He wondered if maybe this man hated Jews and might stab him or something even worse.

"This here," the man said, slowly turning the knife over in his hands to show David how sharp the blade was, and making David swallow hard, "this one here is $8.00 including the tax. More than you have." David's face fell.

"Is there one for seven dollars and fifteen cents?"

"Afraid not, but I'll tell you what. You look like an honest young man. I'll give it to you for seven dollars and you can pay me the other dollar when you have it. Is that fair?"

David didn't hesitate. "Yes sir. Very."

The store owner wrapped the knife in brown paper.

"Don't forget our agreement now." He put out his hand to shake on it. David had never touched the hand of someone not Jewish, but he tentatively reached out letting the man's long fingered hand engulf all of his and shook it.

Bounding out the door, he ran home with his prize tucked under his coat.

***

"Dovey, vee bistu? Where were you? Your father and Adam waited for you to go to shul. I was worried."

David slowly took the brown paper wrapped package from under his coat and handed it to his mother.

"Vas is dis?" she said, sitting down at the table and pulling off the paper. "From where?" she asked, examining the knife from all different angles. Her eyes brimming.

He told her about the man in the store just as his father came through the kitchen door. Malka slid the paper over the knife, but too late. It had already been seen. Zev narrowed his eyes and glancing from one face to the other quickly assessed the situation.

"David, you bought this? ON SHABBOS? And you didn't have money for tires?" His jaw tightened as he walked away shaking his head. David trembled. He knew the Pa was angrier than he had ever seen him.

Later, from his bedroom, he heard his parents arguing. "He has to be punished Malka. If he disrespects everything we've taught him, what will he be like when he gets older." It wasn't a question.

Adam felt badly. He knew his brother had a good heart, but sometimes he acted in haste without thinking. "I wish you would have told me. The knife could have waited another day." Ruth stuck her nose into the room. She had little sympathy for David. Ma was always spoiling him and secretly she wished she had been the one to buy the knife for her mother.

"You're really going to get it this time. I've never seen the Pa so angry," she smirked.

"If you have nothing good to say, get out Ruth, and shut the door behind you," Adam said, seeing the fear cross David's face. David ran to his bed and pulled the covers over his head.

Adam sat on the end of the bed trying to think what would be the best way to resolve the situation – maybe he could make a case for David. 'He's only eleven – didn't you ever do anything thoughtless when you were his age?' he spoke to himself rationalizing – although when the Pa was in this mood, he wasn't sure he would get the sentence out before... the door was flung open. David peeked out from the cover, face pale as the sheet.

"Get my belt, David," Zev said, entering the bedroom – he swiped the cover off in a whoosh and dropped it on the floor. David swallowed hard. There was no use trying to wriggle out of his punishment. He knew what he did was wrong, but his mother... "I don't know where it is," he said, his voice tremulous. His teeth had started to chatter just like the wind-up ones in the joke store that he and Adam always laughed about.

"On the chair in my bedroom." Zev's face was set like stone.

David seeing there was no escape bolted by him trying to decide if he should make a run for the front door – but what use. He would have to come home sometime. He could hear Adam and his Ma pleading with the Pa not to do it. His father boomed, "ENOUGH!" and everything became silent.

In his parent's bedroom he looked at the hated belt hanging on the back of the chair. *What if I throw it out the window? It will only be worse if he has to go fetch it. Better to get it over with.* His mother entered the room with several schmatas in her hands.

"Here Dovey, quickly, put these on." He slid the three tops on one over the other. Picking up the belt he walked slowly back to his room. The Pa was coming towards him in the hallway.

"What took you so long?" His voice was eerily flat – his eyes were like black marbles. David couldn't answer, a stone had formed in his throat. Seizing the belt, Zev clamped onto David's arm and began thrashing him. "You know why I have to do this, don't you?" Zev said, breathing hard in between thwacks. "It's for your own good. You're going to end up a bum if you don't learn…"

Ruth and Adam covered their ears and ran to the kitchen. Malka stood cringing at the sound of David's cries. Finally, she had enough. Charging over to Zev, she beat on his broad back with her fists yelling, "stop it Zev! He did something good! STOP!" She reached for the belt and pulled back on it trying to yank it out of his hands. Zev pushed her off, but dropped the belt and stormed out of the room. "And forget about the hockey game!" he snarled, slamming his bedroom door behind him. The three tee-shirts he had put on had taken a lot of the sting out of the beating, but what hurt even more than that was hearing his father say he wouldn't be going to the hockey game.

David couldn't believe his ears. He was crushed. A customer had given his father three free hockey tickets and he and Adam had been so excited that the Pa was taking them to see the Detroit Red Wings play against the Canadiens at the Montreal Forum. He had bragged to all his friends. For days the forum was all David could think about – he had never seen it, but his friends told him it was huge inside and that the players looked like little ants way down on the ice. He hoped the tickets they had might be closer to the ice so he could see his favorite player, Jean Beliveau, and possibly even shake his hand, although maybe that was too much to hope for. He and Adam had both been crossing the days off a calendar and now he wouldn't be going. It was too much to bear. He felt a deep sense of despair inside. Would he always be this powerless? Why did the Pa hate him so much? Why were rules more important to the Pa than seeing Ma happy? He let out a huge sigh and gave a shudder trying to hold back the tears.

Malka came into the bedroom enfolding David in her arms. He felt her softness and warmth, but something had shut down inside him. He wasn't going to cry, ever again. What good did tears do anyway. Nothing changed. Being hurt is just part of life – *but when I get bigger, nobody is ever going to hurt me again.*

"It's okay Dovey. You did good. Hush now," she said, stroking his hair. Malka understood Zev's anger came from his disappointment in himself, but she couldn't forgive him for taking it out on David.

Pushing away from his mother, he asked, "Why does he hate me Ma? I try everything I know to be a good son."

"He doesn't hate you Dovey. He hates himself and his weakness."

When Adam saw his father leave through the kitchen door, he went into the bedroom to console David.

"Don't cry little brother. Maybe he'll change his mind. There's still a couple of weeks before the game." Adam rubbed David's back gently. "I wish I would have known what you were going to do. I would have advised you to wait and we could have gone together on Monday."

The next week, with Ruth at her friend's house, Malka took the boys to Levitts Kosher Smoked Meat on the Main to make up for the punishment in a small way.

Opening the door and ushering them in, she said, "go Dovey and get a table." She turned to the counter to place her order. "One sandwich please, three glasses of water." The counterman having noted the woman with the two boys in the hand-me-down clothes nodded, carved up the meat and threw on a few extra slices. Carefully she removed a five dollar bill from her purse smoothing it out and paid at the cash. Adam counted the change and taking the tray with the sandwich and three waters he sat down at the table next to David, across from his mother. Malka reached into her purse, retrieved three squares of wax paper and placed a piece in front of each of them. Giving the boys a full slice of bread, she divided the tender fragrant meat between them, keeping the smallest portion for herself. "And after lunch Dovey, we'll walk with you to the hardware store and you'll make a last payment to the nice man a quarter."

"Oh David," Jorie said passionately. "I can see why you love your mother so much. What a good woman she is. But please tell me you had some happy times. You did, didn't you?" Jorie asked hopefully.

"I guess we had some good times...Once someone gave me a pop-gun as a present. I was ecstatic and thought I could never receive a better gift, but money was always very tight and the important thing for my father was to make the mortgage payments so we wouldn't be homeless – if we couldn't afford food, at least we always had a roof over our heads. Sometimes I think back and I wonder how my mother managed to feed us so that we never went to bed without something in our stomachs. And now that I think about it, our fun came from being outside with our friends. We were good at inventing games out of nothing. When chestnuts fell from the trees on neighboring streets, we'd drill a hole in the nut, thread a length of string through it and try to hit each other's nut until we broke the other guys and declared ourselves champion nut cracker." David chuckled. "For some reason I thought soaking my nut in vinegar would make it harder. Where that information came from, I have no idea. And of course there was always marbles. The city had some kind of little covers in the sidewalks, the width of an orange. We'd remove them and use the hole for the marble pocket. But, Chinese auctions were the most exciting. We always hoped we'd find a treasure of jewels or a pocket-full of forgotten money."

"What the heck is a Chinese auction?" Jorie asked.

"It's an auction where they put bags, suitcases and items that were never picked up by passengers on the train – you bid on them and take your chances on the contents. David thought back to a particular time and began to talk about it.

"I can't wait to see what he comes home with," Ruth said excitedly to Adam, "this is supposed to be the biggest one they've ever had." Adam was studying as usual, hunched over the kitchen table. He was always studying and usually didn't like to be disturbed, but this time he sat up and pushed the book away.

"Yeah, last year there were some pretty good clothes." Checking the time on the wall clock, Adam said, "he should be home any minute. I'll wait for the Pa downstairs and help him carry the suitcases up. David, come with me."

David turned to go eagerly, but Malka had a hold of him. "Zei schtil Dovey, stay still," she said, keeping David standing in front of her.

Five minutes later, the kitchen door opened. The Pa was huffing and puffing from climbing the three flights of stairs. He and Adam placed two fat suitcases and a duffel bag on the scuffed linoleum by the wood stove. Ruth plunked down on the floor, grabbed the duffel bag and began rummaging through the items.

"Ruth, make your father a glass of tea." Ruth scrambled up and put the kettle on and rushed back to empty the duffel bag.

Malka was sewing a button on David's shirt as he stood in front of her. He tried twisting around to see the excitement. "Zei schtil Dovey – another minute."

He started to spit out the piece of thread he was chewing on. "Ma, every time you sew my buttons, why do you make me chew this thread anyway?"

"Mir zollen nit farnayen der saychel," Adam piped up, "superstition, so she doesn't sew up your common sense.

You better keep chewing that thread little brother," he chided David with a mischievous grin.

"Ruth..." Malka said, leaning over and handing Ruth a needle and a new length of thread. Ruth closed one eye, zeroing in on the hole and quickly threaded it, handing it back to her mother. Malka began rhythmically shoving the needle in and out on the third button.

"Look what I found! A really nice ring in a pocket!" Ruth exclaimed.

"Hah," David couldn't contain himself any longer. He pulled away from his mother leaving the needle and thread dangling from his shirt. Snatching the ring from Ruth's hand. "A piece of junk," as he slipped it on his middle finger.

"Give it back! Ma, make him give it back."

"Adam, sort through the clothes and keep what you like. The rest will go with the Pa to the country." They always hoped to find a package of money that would make them rich, but it wasn't to be this time.

"Did you ever find anything of value?" Jorie asked.

"Usually we lost money," he said with a rueful grin.

"Will there be anything else, sir? We'll be closing in ten minutes," the waiter asked, placing the check on the table.

Jorie looked around. She and David were the only two left in the restaurant. "I didn't even notice how late it was I was so interested in what you were saying."

She was deeply touched by the emotion of David's story. She resisted an urge to put her arms around him; he seemed so self-contained she didn't dare.

Conflicted thoughts swirled through David's head. He was flattered that Jorie had been interested in his life and hadn't judged him, but at the same time he had a hollow feeling, nervous from having laid himself bare, for exposing his family troubles, but also, strangely freed – he felt somehow lighter.

After that evening, David, against his better judgment, found himself more and more seeking out Jorie's company. He knew he was putting them both in a no-win situation. Several times he had been to her parent's house to help her move some bigger items into her newly rented apartment. Her parents didn't seem concerned that they were getting closer. *Could it really be they don't care that I'm Jewish?* He found it hard to believe, but what if he allowed himself to believe it and then they turned on him. It would be ugly and painful. But, he reasoned with himself… just take them at face value. Not everybody hates Jews…still…it was always there in the back of his mind. *What if…*

Chapter Eleven

Owning a horse for pleasure. David couldn't even imagine it. Jorie kept a horse on her friend, Annie's farm, and she wanted to take him riding. He wasn't brought up to pursue frivolous gratification. Study, work, save. *You never know what life will throw at you. You always have to be prepared.*

Since his divorce David had moved back home. To silence. His father stopped talking to him, would not even be in the same room with him. Still, he was pleased to be able to take some of the pressure off his parents by contributing part of his salary. And he was happy to spoil his mother with the few things he knew she would never buy for herself.

Jorie wanted to take him to the farm to 'meet' her horse on Saturday, but that was impossible. He wasn't sure why he had moved back home, having to live again under his father's strict dictates, but it didn't matter, either way he still carried too much guilt to drive in a car on Shabbos.

They set out Sunday morning. The day was sunshine bright and the air crisp. "A perfect riding day; no horseflies to bother us," Jorie said. "You're going to love riding, David," she chirped. When he was young, his uncle would hoist him up bareback onto Freidela in her stall or let him feed the horse her oats, so he wasn't exactly afraid of horses but it was another thing to actually ride one on a trail.

As soon as they pulled into the parking lot, Jorie bounded out of the car and calling David, raced to the barn. Sometimes David found her enthusiasm child-like. It touched him in a way that he found endearing and he wished he could be as excited about everything as she was.

"Doesn't the barn smell wonderful? I wish they could bottle it," Jorie said, inhaling with a feigned swoon.

David pulled a face and laughed. "I can just imagine the marketing campaign. Step right up ladies and gentlemen. Be the first to lay down your hard earned dollars for a bottle of horse shit smell."

"What shit-smell?" She gave him a disparaging look. "What do you know. It's horses and hay and leather and simply heavenly," she smirked at him while opening the stall door. Putting a lead rope on Mardi she led him into the aisle and attached the cross-ties to his halter.

"I know one thing, I wouldn't be the one to invest in it."

"Oh, poo. Hand me that brush please," pointing to the open tack box. "Isn't Mardi Gras beautiful David?" she said, stroking the horse's neck with obvious affection and pride. "I could have moved out of my parent's house sooner if I sold him and not had to pay his board, but I just couldn't part with him. I mean, how often do you see a golden buckskin with four black stockings and confirmation like this? And he's just the sweetest," she said, kissing his soft nose.

David looked at her quizzically. He had no answer. To him, apart from different colors, horses all looked the same.

"I ride English, but I'll put a western saddle for you on Blackjack. He's very gentle; you're not nervous are you?" He was nervous, but seeing as she was always so confident, he certainly wasn't going to let her know.

They left the paddock and rode side by side along a wagon path. It's not unpleasant, David thought. Different. Spiritually freeing in an odd sort of way, the powerful movement of the horse under him, the quietness of the wooded path. Clopping along, Jorie turned to face him.

"I'm an avid reader David, but your story is so much better than any books I've ever read."

He wasn't sure how he felt about his life being compared to 'a story'. The living it was so much more, more difficult, but he understood she didn't mean it in a superficial way.

"What about your life? Tell me something about your childhood."

"Mine? Not nearly as interesting as yours, I can assure you. I have nothing to complain about. Christmases were always special when my grandfather was alive. One in particular I remember... Grandpa was a Kiwanis member and they would rent a huge room in a ritzy hotel where maybe fifty Kiwanis families would each have a long table and have their whole families there. Way at the front of the room, and when you're nine-years-old, the room seemed enormous – Santa would come down a faux chimney and seat himself on a throne next to a big bag full of presents. He would reach into the bag, take out a gift wrapped package and then call each child's name and you had to walk up the long red carpet in front of everybody to get your gift.

I had been so excited my first time. I remember I was wearing a short taffeta dress with several crinolines underneath, white ankle socks and black patent leather shoes and my curly hair was held on either side by two pink bows. When Santa called my name, walking up the red carpet seemed to take forever and I just thought I was a princess for sure. My poofy dress swung back and forth and I felt everyone's eyes on me. It was very exciting and then he gave me my gift and I had to walk all the way back to our table. I remember blushing the whole way with a big smile on my face."

"What did the gift turn out to be?"

"A wide sterling silver bangle bracelet engraved on the inside with my name. I still have it. But, the downturn of that day was when they ran out of the little browned roastie potatoes right before they came to my brother and I. You would've thought it was the end of the world the way we carried on," she laughed.

"I have to admit, looking back, we were very spoiled. My parents took us on a lot of trips to fun places and at Easter they would always rent a chalet in the Laurentian Mountains with some other friends of theirs. If there was snow, we would ski and when we were little, they would hide chocolate Easter eggs and treats outside and we'd hunt for them.

Birthdays, my mother always took us and several of our friends to Piazza Tomaso restaurant where Uncle Tom would perform magic tricks for us. I can still taste the birthday cake — it was the most delicious thing ever!

And then when I was really little, my grandparents would take me, being the first grandchild, to a restaurant where the attraction was to let children bottle feed a real live pink baby pig on the table. Looking back, little did I know, cute little piggy was probably going to be on the menu shortly after," she groaned.

Suddenly she stopped talking and glanced at David. He had an inscrutable, mildly amused look on his face.

"What? Why are you looking like that? — I talked too much?"

"Not at all. It just confirms what I've known all along. Our worlds are sooo far apart."

"So what! It doesn't mean we can't form our own world going forward."

They walked along in silence while Jorie tried to figure out what was going on in his mind.

"Before we were interrupted in the restaurant, you mentioned your father had brought home a surprise. You never finished or told me what it was."

1953

One Friday afternoon in winter, just before Shabbos, the kitchen door opened and the Pa came in huffing and puffing after lugging a large box up the three floors.

'RCA' was printed in big black letters on the side.

"It's a television!" Ruth and David shouted in unison jumping up and down. Even the staid Adam was excited. They had wanted a television set forever. Almost all of their friends had one. "We'll be able to watch Hockey Night in Canada!" David exclaimed.

The Pa took his time unboxing it and placed it carefully on a wooden table. He didn't plug it in. They heard him telling Malka that a customer had given it to him in lieu of payment he didn't have.

"It's Shabbos. You can't turn it on until Saturday night. Farshtaist? You understand." It wasn't a question the way the Pa said it.

Zev handed Malka what was left of the weekly money he earned from peddling and went into the kitchen for a glass of tea. She placed a plate of roast chicken, two knishes and tzimmes in front of him which he attacked ravenously. After eating, and a shot glass of schnapps – his only indulgence to himself every Friday, he was just too worn out to go to shul and went into his bedroom and shut the door.

It wasn't long before they heard him snoring heavily.

"Please Ma, turn it on," David pleaded. Three pairs of eyes looked at her with excited anticipation. They had so few luxuries, Malka found it hard to deny them anything in her power. She gave a faint nod. David raced to plug it in and his mother turned the knob.

"Keep the sound low," she said, with a finger to her lips. The Plouffe Family came to life on the screen. Mesmerized at once, the three kids sat down on the floor in rapt attention. Suddenly, POOF! The Plouffes disappeared in a whirl of gray and white. The screen went black.

"The tube blew," Adam said in a flat voice. David looked incredulous.

"Turn it off, quickly, and tomorrow we'll ask the Pa to turn it on and he'll think he did it," David said. "Maybe his customer will take it back and give us a new one."

"Dreaming again, little brother?" Adam said, feeling his own sense of disappointment at the loss.

The next day the Pa was furious. He decreed it was a punishment for having used it on Shabbos and that was the end of TV.

***

Later in the month David sat in the Yeshiva daydreaming as the rabbi droned on and on. Any good parts in the Gemora referencing 's-e-x', he and his friends agreed were hastily by-passed. He glanced out the schoolroom window watching a bird land on a leafless branch and wished he had wings and could fly away from the Yeshiva to somewhere a lot more interesting. He noticed a figure, his father, trudging down the street, the bitter March wind whipping the thin black material of his coat around his legs. One hand was holding his hat to his head and the other arm was clamped close to his side. The Pa had definitely aged lately and it frightened David. What would the family do if something happened to him?

David shivered and his stomach grumbled – he had forgotten to bring his lunch. Heating wasn't a priority of The Beth Israel, where he studied Hebrew on Sundays. Heat cost money. Asking to be excused, he left the classroom and went down the hallway to meet his father at the locked front door. Stepping inside, Zev reached under his armpit and handed David a tightly wrapped veal chop, "your mother said to keep it warm. Here, a pen and pencil Nadler gave me when I ran into him. He thinks we have money for insurance." Zev grumbled as he walked back out into the frigid air.

**

With the arrival of Passover drawing near, things became hectic around the flat. Every minute they could spare, Ruth, Adam and David carried crate after crate of grapes up to the third floor, exhausting themselves. They stored them in the dilapidated enclosed back porch with it's dirty mullioned windows overlooking the laneway. Wiping away the grime with the side of his fist, as far as David could see, hanging laundry crisscrossed all the way down the whole back alley.

Then came the magical part – making grapes into wine. After school, the kids picked the stems off, washed the grapes and threw them into a barrel on the porch. David often wondered if the rickety floor would collapse from the extra weight, it groaned and creaked, but never gave way.

The contained air in the shed seemed five times colder than the air outside. Freezing, in only his underwear, goosebumps running up his spine, David climbed into the barrel and stomped the cold grapes until all the red juice was pressed out. Ruth and Adam doubled over laughing gleefully as he clambered out, his skinny legs stained purple almost to his crotch.

After that, Malka began the process of skimming the shim every four or five days. The sugar was added and two weeks later, the wine was ready to be bottled; a time consuming job. David watched as his mother carefully inserted a cloth down into the neck of a bottle and slowly added the wine to strain. After that, they all took turns until the wine was fully decanted into bottles and sealed.

The rabbi of the shul knew David's family well and that they kept a Kosher house so most of the bottles were sold to the Synagogue, but there were always a few left over to sell to the neighbors and Malka was especially glad to have the extra money for a special treat. It meant steak and French fries for everyone on Sunday.

***

"Dovey, get the chicken and take it to the Shohet."

"I don't want to, Ma." He hated when his mother brought the live chicken home from the market.

Grousing to himself he pulled back the shower curtain. There was the poor chicken regarding him with her beady eyes, cocking her head this way and that. He tried to grab her but she was having none of it. Squawking loudly she raced slipping and sliding around the tub. Finally, dropping a thin towel over her he scooped her up.

Walking along the street with the chicken under his arm, he ran into some friends who joined him. Crossing to the other side, he saw a horse and wagon full of junk round the corner. His heart dropped. *Uncle Levi.* None of his friends had an uncle with a horse and wagon. They all drove cars. *Don't stop! Don't stop!* Sure enough, Uncle Levi pulled up beside them.

"Dovey – how are you? Going to the shohet I see. Would you and your friends like a ride?"

His friends looked excited at the chance to ride on the wagon and pet the horse, but David didn't notice. He was too embarrassed. "No Uncle Levi. It's not much farther. We can walk."

"Okay then. Come see me some time." He saw the sad face on his uncle as he gave a click to the horse and Freidela walked on. David felt totally ashamed and terribly guilty. But he wasn't sure why. Ashamed that his uncle didn't drive a car or ashamed and guilty for letting his father influence him. His uncle never had children and ever since David's father had decided they should sell the tenement building, he and Levi had fought about the price and his father had forbidden the children from seeing their uncle.

Blackjack suddenly stopped and arched his back. David looked at Jorie questioningly.

"It's alright. He's just making a pooper."

"I'm sorry."

"Oh, it's okay. Horses are used to doing it while they're being ridden."

David smirked and pulled a face. "No, I'm not sorry about that! I'm sorry that I must be boring you. I don't remember ever talking this much in my life."

"David, trust me. I'll let you know when you're boring me. What happened after that and what about your little sister? You've never mentioned her." Jorie was totally intrigued by the difference in his upbringing and hers. He had definitely been telling the truth when he said they came from completely different backgrounds. She suddenly felt very spoiled and guilty that she never thought beyond herself and her own desires.

"My little sister died. They said it was 'crib death'. It took a big toll on my mother." David glanced away. "It took a big toll on the whole family," he said softly.

They rode on in silence for a while before Jorie said, "I'm so sorry." So many hardships in this family and wished she hadn't asked because she saw the pain in

David's eyes. She so much wanted to make him laugh, instead she had made him feel sad.

A few minutes later David rallied himself and continued. "Some punks tried to set the back alley sheds on fire so my parents borrowed some money from the Hebrew Free Loan, and we moved to a different section of the city." He chuckled a little.

"What's so funny?"

"Well, after we got the money, five thousand dollars in cash, a vast fortune at the time, my father sent my mother and I to deposit it in the bank. She couldn't read or write and me being eleven or twelve-years-old, what did I know? But when she went to the teller and took all the money out of her purse, a man standing behind her told her she should give it to him and he would invest it for her and make her lots of money. I could see the indecision on her face so I jumped in between them and told him I would yell for the police if he didn't leave us alone. He backed off then."

"What's a Hebrew Free Loan, David?"

"It's an interest-free loan they give to people going through hard financial times. My parents paid it all back little by little."

Suddenly David blurted out, "Don't think my father is a cruel person. He isn't. He's just a beaten-down soul. Both my parents had to flee from their home countries and start over with absolutely nothing. Can you imagine having to learn a new language…my father speaks five languages, but for my mother, not so easy. They had to learn to navigate a new country, find shelter and jobs. He's always worked hard, the best he knows how, to provide for the family. And I often wonder what his childhood was like…what his father was like with him. From some of the stories Uncle Levi told us, before they came here, in the old country, they had it really tough as kids. We never knew our grandparents. And my mother, even though she didn't have an education, her greatest pride was in feeding her family and keeping us safe. They sacrificed a great deal for us."

The two horses came close together as the path narrowed and Jorie impulsively reached over and squeezed his hand. He entwined his fingers with hers and they rode on a ways hand in hand. She wondered if he felt her heart reaching out to him.

"You really think the world of your mother," Jorie said softly, thinking about her relationship with her own parents. She automatically loved them, they were her parents after all, but they were just there. Her father made a good living and they provided her and her brother with whatever they needed. Her parents had never struggled for anything, or if they did, she had never heard about it. Oh sure, they went through some rough spots, mostly inflicted on themselves from too much partying…but never 'struggled'. Or maybe they did and just kept it to themselves. She'd have to think about that. It was strange to imagine her parents as 'real' people.

Arriving back at the stable, Jorie untacked the horses and carried the saddles into the tack room. David came in behind her, framing her in between his arms, his hands pressed against the wall. Leaning in, he kissed her on the lips. A pillow kiss, so soft and inviting that when he stopped, she almost fell over. She never imagined a kiss could be so entrancing, so all consuming.

"But, wait a minute," she said, ducking out from under his arm. Reality had broken the spell. "David you said you were getting a divorce. You never told me if you did. Are you divorced?"

"That's what you were thinking of when I kissed you? Stick a knife in my ego," he said, putting a hand to his heart. "To answer your question, yes, we're divorced. There was no contest. She admitted to the affair and got her 'get'."

"A 'get'? What's a get?"

"Someday we'll have a talk about the laws of Judaism, which we probably couldn't cover in a lifetime, but for the reader's digest version, a get is what a husband gives his wife to facilitate her being able to remarry in the Jewish faith.

"Did she give you a get?"

David's mouth formed a wry smile. "Only the husband gives it to the wife."

"And if he doesn't want to?"

"Well then, it's turned over to the Beit Din to make further determination."

"Beit din… you mean like a jury?" Jorie pulled in her chin. "Not to be insulting or anything, but this sounds very medieval."

He knew she didn't mean any offense, but this was just the thing he had been wary of.

"Look," he said, putting a distance between them. "I told you at the beginning you wouldn't understand the world I come from, didn't I?"

"But I want to David. I'm going to get some books from the library and read about Judaism. It's just that since I was a teenager I stopped believing in religions. I see them as greedy corporations, run by men who want control over people's minds and money and get it by scaring them with hellfire or guilting them to death with religious brain-washing jargon. I saw a documentary once about volcanos and it made me think that perhaps early people seeing fire coming out of the earth, associated that with hell being 'down there'. I mean, it would be logical for a primitive mind to think that and the myth would follow down through history for unscrupulous men to take advantage of."

"Well, I respect your logic," he said, without rancor, "but a lot of the Jewish laws that were made way back then were made to protect people from illness by thinkers ahead of their time – for example, not eating pork. In the days of old, there was no refrigeration. Just that alone probably saved a lot of Jewish lives from dying of trichinosis."

"But that was then, and this is now."
He could see he wasn't going to gain any ground in a short time. "Well, let's sum it up this way. When you're brought up all your life to follow and believe in a certain religious doctrine and all your friends and neighbors believe the same, sometimes it's difficult to find your own path."

Jorie resolved to question Hella more about the intriguing parts of Judaism. Even though Hella didn't practice, she had been brought up in the faith – at least until her mother died.

Chapter Twelve

"My parents have rented a cottage on Duck Lake for the summer. They're away this coming weekend and said I could use it. I would love for you to come David. There's plenty of spare bedrooms," she quickly added so he wouldn't think she was planning on seducing him. "Hella will be there with her boyfriend... "

"I won't come for the weekend, but I'll drive up Saturday night. Might be late"

Disappointed, she managed to say, "great, you'll have a good time, you'll see. Bring your swim trunks."

After Shabbos finished Saturday night, David jumped into his car and following Jorie's directions and a two hour drive, he arrived at the lake. It was dark, but from what he could see, the place looked sprawling and well lit up. He saw a group of people sitting around a fire pit by the edge of the lake and hesitantly walked towards them. *What am I doing here? I don't belong with these people. Keep moving. Relax.* He had to admit to himself, the balmy night air, the crackling fire surrounded by silhouettes in chairs and the sound of the crickets was intoxicating his senses.

Jorie spotted him and jumped up running through the dewy grass towards him.

"David! I'm so glad you came; I was beginning to get worried. Here, come, let me introduce you," she said, taking him by the hand. "You already know Peter and Vicky from the office. Jordan Grossman and his wife Ellie – they have a place down the road – Hella, you're familiar with and her boyfriend Marcel."

Everyone welcomed David – the men shook hands. He was still in shock to see his old friend Marcel sitting there. They had lost touch over the years but he was happy to see a familiar face.

"Can I get you a drink?"

"Whatever you're having."

"Here," Jorie said reaching into a cooler and handing him a cold beer at the same time dragging over an Adirondack chair next to her.

Grossman...he, they, must be Jewish. He felt a little better knowing there were some lantsman, countrymen, other than himself. He didn't really consider Hella Jewish for some reason. But Marcel?...that was a pleasant surprise.

Peter picked up a guitar and strummed a few tunes, the fire crackled, mesmerizing sparks shot up into the black night sky to join the stars. The lake water lapped against the shoreline. It was peaceful, David thought. And nice. *But I'm so out of my element. Just relax. If you don't have a good time, or you feel uncomfortable, you can always get in your car and drive home. I hope they don't serve traif for breakfast.*

Marcel came over pulling a chair up next to David.

"You're the last person I expected to run into," he said, grinning.

"Well, we're on the same page there. How long have you and Hella been dating?"

Marcel was handsome in an odd sort of way. His nose was flattened like a boxers, but his manner and personality were relaxed and calming.

"Just about a year. She's quite a girl. Her real name was Helen, but she changed it to Hella and I think it suits her personality. She's a handful, but you couldn't find a better person when you need someone on your side. How's the family doing?"

At the mention of 'family', David's guilt meter went up. What would the Pa say if he saw David carousing...

"I ran into your sister Ruth some time ago. She said you had gotten married. And yet, here you are." Marcel looked at him quizzically. David grimaced. "Over so soon? Got it. Why don't we get together back in town and catch up? So what brings you here?"

"I came alone. Jorie and I work together and she invited me."

"Aha. Oh, oh. Does this mean you and she...?"

"Nothing like that. Just friends."

"C'mon David. You wouldn't come all this way if you weren't interested a little bit."

"Unfortunately you're right. And you know how complicated this can make her life and mine?"

"Jesus man, when I saw you here, I thought you had let go of all that stuff."

"Not so easy my friend. I'm trying. I want to be free to make my own decisions, but there are always consequences, unpleasant ones and you know what I'm saying is true."

Car headlights coming up the long drive way distracted them.

Jorie had been talking to Hella and Ellie when she saw the silhouette of a man striding across the lawn. As he got closer, she looked aghast to see that it was Jace. Jumping up, she ran to catch him before he came any closer.

"What are you doing here?"

"Your brother Rick told me you were having a party and I was disappointed I wasn't included. I haven't heard from you in weeks and since you're not returning my calls, well…here I am."

"And I see you've been drinking. Well, where ever you came from, you better just go back."

Jorie was panicking. She didn't want David to think she was still seeing Jace and she certainly didn't want a scene.

The darkness provided a cloak over them and she hoped David hadn't noticed.

"I just want to talk to you for a few minutes. Can you give me that much for old times sake?" His voice took on an edge.

He could become belligerent and she thought it might be better to cooperate, listen to what he has to say and get him gone.

"Come over here," she said, leading him further into the darkness and away from the lights of the house. "Well?"

"I've missed you, Baby."

"So that's what you came to say? Okay, you said it. Now go back to where ever it is you're staying."

"Don't be like that. I thought maybe I could stay here…for the night."

"Absolutely not. All the bedrooms are accounted for."

"You're hard Jorie. You know that. What's happened to you? Are you so angry with me that you've forgotten what we had together?"

"Jace, you're the one who broke up with me. You only seem to remember what 'we had' when you're between girlfriends or drunk. Well, I've moved on. You have to go."

Whether it was feeling sorry for him or some feelings still deeply buried inside, she felt herself weakening at his sad face. Suddenly he grabbed her head and planted a deep kiss forcing his tongue between her teeth. She broke away. Her heart pounding. Now she remembered. This isn't about me. He just wants what he wants when he wants it. And this time it wasn't going to work.

Pushing away hard on his chest, she said in a loud voice, "stop it you idiot! You better leave right now before things get ugly. There's several guys here who will escort you out if you don't."

Over by the fire, David, Marcel and Jordan got up and walked a little ways towards Jorie and Jace.

"I think that's the guy she was dating, but I thought it was over," David said.

"C'mon, let's go and see what's going on," said Marcel, taking the lead.

David hesitated. Right from the beginning he told himself he didn't want to get into a competition. A relationship with her wasn't going to work anyway, so what was the point of trying to win her over. *On the other hand, why did I come here?* The attraction he felt for her was undeniable but attraction isn't everything...*or am I just telling myself that?*

From twenty feet away they saw him force a kiss on her and heard her response. David suddenly had the urge to punch the guy in the face.

Seeing the three men striding toward him...Jace released her but didn't make a move to leave.

"Everything okay, Jorie?" Marcel asked.

"Could you guys please escort this rude person to his car," Jorie nodded at David and Marcel.

"I'm going," Jace said angrily. "Just remember what we had Jorie. You'll come around and it'll be too late. You'll see."

Giving a sigh of exasperation, Jorie rolled her eyes. "Just go."

After the confrontation was over, everyone drifted away for the night and Jorie showed David to his room. The house was rambling, but charmingly appointed.

"I hope you'll be comfortable David. Good-night, see you in the morning." Jorie leaned up kissing him on the cheek and turned to go.

"Jorie?" he grabbed her arm and pulled her back towards him. "What you said is true? You and him, you're finished?"

"One hundred percent!"

"I hope so." With that, he put his arms around her and kissed her on the lips. Gentle but forceful; she was mesmerized by the feeling and didn't want it to stop. Warm waves of sensation flooded through her body. Letting her go suddenly, they stood apart before he turned her around and pushed her off in the direction of her room.

Later, after everyone had gone to bed, Jorie heard a soft knock on her bedroom door. *It's David...I knew he would come.* Throwing the covers off, she ran to the door.

"Hella?"

"Well, don't look so disappointed."

"I'm not, I just thought..."

"You thought it was Mr. Freezie, right? Sorry about that, but I thought we should talk," she said, plopping down on the bottom of the bed and pulling her knees up under her night gown.

"He's not really cold, you know. He's just bound-up in some kind of battle with himself." Jorie propped herself up on her pillows. "What a jerk Jace turned out to be. If I had any feelings left for him, they're gone now."

"And transferred to David?"

Jorie looked down at her hands, her red polished nails spread out on the white duvet. "Maybe – but it's different with David, Hella. He's...I don't know how to describe it, but I see something much deeper in him –Jace was all flash with nothing underneath the hood. Or maybe I just want something different. Am I maturing? Could that actually be it?" she said, crossing her eyes and sticking her tongue out the side of her mouth.

"It's not going to work, you know. You're in for a painful uphill battle," Hella said gently.

Startled at the unusual softness of her words, Jorie squinted and pulled back her chin. "Why are you saying that?"

"David comes from a religious family. You have no clue how much control they have over his life. They're never going to accept you. You're asking for a whole heap of bad news and I'm not relishing seeing you get hurt."

"Well then, why did he come here?" Jorie said, a bit incensed at the implication, after just coming down from such an enchanting kiss.

"I'm not denying there's an attraction between you, but think about it. Has he ever agreed to see you on Friday night? No, because it's Shabbos and he probably spends it at his parents house. Why do you think he arrived here so late on Saturday?"

"Why?" Jorie asked with a sinking feeling.

"Because religious Jews stop working on Fridays at sundown and stay that way until after sundown on Saturdays. They walk to synagogue because they don't drive, don't turn on lights, don't cook – basically don't do anything, besides sleep or pray."

"That sounds so, so medieval," Jorie sputtered.

"Medieval it may sound, but that's how David was brought up...and that's just a very wee small little piece of it" she said, emphasizing it between her thumb and forefinger – "does that sound like something you want to deal with? You're always going to be the 'unwanted' – they might even sit shiva for him if he takes up with you."

"Shiva? What's shiva?"

"That my dear girl is when they consider him dead – to them anyway."

"But I'm a nice girl from a decent family – I'm sure they'll change when they see that I don't mean him any harm – that I really care about him?" David's earlier words sprung to her mind. 'You have no concept about my world.'

"You're dreaming in technicolor. Even if you were the queen of England, you aren't Jewish and that's that. Besides, we've talked about religion many times and I know your feelings on that subject. 'It's a male dominated corporation, yadda, yadda —' "

"But I wouldn't try and un-convert him. He could practice his religion all he wants."

"And if he wants **you** to convert and keep kosher?" Hella already anticipated the coming question. "Remember I told you once when I had a friend visit my mother's place and the friend went to use a spoon to dish out ice-cream? How my mother shrieked because it was a 'meat spoon' and not a 'dairy' one?"

"Yes, I do remember, but I kind of thought that your mother was just a bit neurotic about cutlery."

"No, no, no, my friend. There are meat dishes and dairy dishes along with cutlery and every other thing in the kitchen that has to be kept separate."

"Wow!" Jorie thought about that. "Seems like a lot of work for the woman, not to mention you have to have a lot of space. What if I studied and converted?"

"Whoa, I think you're getting ahead of yourself. You haven't a clue about what's involved, besides, you and David have only had what, three or four dates?"

"He met my parents and ate at our house and seemed fine afterward."

Hella pondered that piece of information. "Well, I guess he really does like you. That must have been very difficult for him."

"Now that you mention it, he was uncomfortable, but to his credit, he didn't let on."

"Well Jor Jor, don't say I didn't warn you. In the words of Bette Davis, 'fasten your seatbelt. It's going to be a bumpy ride.' I'll see you in the morning girlfriend." With that she jumped off the bed, flounced to the door throwing up her nighty to expose her bare bum, blew Jorie a kiss and left for her own room.

Turning off the light, Jorie tossed and turned thinking of why things have to be so complicated – and maybe Hella was right – maybe it was more than she wanted to take on. Jace's mother had loved her. Had called her after their break-up and said how sorry she was. That she had been a good influence on him. Why wouldn't David's parents like her as much? Hella had given Jorie a lot to think about. It can't possibly be as strict as she says.

***

Sunday morning proved to be a perfect water day. Only 10:00 AM and the air was hot and hazy with humidity. The girls packed a picnic lunch and everyone piled into their cars and drove to the near-by quarry. After climbing over a fence, navigating ankle-twisting rocks and getting attacked by bramble bushes, they came upon an expanse of trodden down grass surrounding a giant crater.

"There are cows pastured in here." Jorie said to David, pointing out several cow pies, "and sometimes a meanish bull, so you might want to keep an eye out. But generally we hear the bull bellowing before he comes into view."

David rolled his eyes. "A bull. Great – good to know." Walking cautiously to the chiseled stone edge he glanced down at the seemingly fathomless water far below. *Terrific! I can take a chance of getting gored by a bull or jumping to my death off this cliff.*

Jorie had stripped off her t-shirt and shorts down to her bathing suit. It was the first time he had seen her, or any woman for that matter, in something so revealing – even in his short marriage, he and Devora had kept themselves modestly covered being that uncomfortable with each other. And religious women were never without a wig or head covering, long skirts, stockings and three-quarter length sleeves. Her suit was a simple one piece blue print, but it outlined her figure in a way that stirred something deep in his loins and took him by surprise, a very pleasant surprise.

"C'mon David!" Jorie yelled as she fearlessly leaped off the twenty foot cliff and plunged into the water, disappearing into the dark green depths. After an anxious breath, staring down at the rippling water, he was relieved when she popped to the surface like a cork. Swimming quickly to the side she nimbly climbed up the rocks back to where David was standing. He was in his bathing trunks and Jorie was surprised to see how muscular he was. She rudely looked him up and down appraisingly.

"Wow! For a Yeshiva boy, you've got quite a build on you," she said admiringly.

David felt heat rise to his face. "Geez! Don't hold anything back Jorie," he said feeling both exposed and pleased at the same time. "I always liked lifting weights, ever since I was a kid, so with my first pay check I bought myself a set." *I'll never be beaten again by anyone* flashed through his mind.

"I can't do it."

"C'mon, I'll hold your hand and we can jump together," she said enthusiastically, pulling him toward the edge.

"Afraid I'm going to have to pass," he said, planting his feet firmly.

"Tsk, alriiiight," she said with a frown, and then making a fast recovery, "well, have you ever been water-skiing?"

"Nope. 'fraid not. Boats and lakes weren't something my father…"

"But you know how to swim don't you?" she interrupted, and then reconsidering, "maybe I should have asked you that before encouraging you to jump."

He gave her an amused smile. "Yes, I learned one summer when we went to Jewish day-camp."

"Good – you'll love water-skiing. It's like walking on water – so much fun!" With that she turned and leaped off the cliff again.

Phew, she has a lot of energy. He found her excitement for life contagious and although it went against everything he had been taught, he wanted to experience some of that carefree feeling. But – and there was always the niggling in the back of his mind. – *for every action, there are consequences and some of those consequences can be devasting.* Always the sword of Damocles hanging over his neck. *What if I ?…How are they going to react…She's going to be hurt, very hurt. Can I choose? Not without causing anger and pain to someone, myself included.* Just recently his sister Ruth had been putting pressure on him to meet her nice Jewish girlfriend.

"Hannah Brownstein, David, you remember her? She's really smart and not too frum."

Just the fact that Ruth mentioned 'not too frum' meant she suspected that David had interests elsewhere and he wasn't going to be taking on another religious girl like his first wife, Devora. There was still the whiff of scandal going around the neighborhood about that.

The girls, refreshed and cool from their swim, spread the sandwiches, salads and drinks onto a blanket while the boys threw around a football.

"David – head's up!" Marcel yelled as he threw the ball towards David. David caught it and hurled it back towards Jordan.

"Good catch," somebody yelled. David's glum thoughts disappeared and he was surprised to realize he was having a good time. *Get out of myself. Stop over-thinking. Let go. Let go.*

"Come and eat," Vicky yelled. Dropping the ball, the guys came running.

Food again. Guilt and anxiety flooded back. He hadn't asked for anything special – didn't want to draw attention to himself for being 'different'. He had seen the packages of cold cuts on the counter. He could feign he was still full from breakfast. Toast, eggs, strawberries. Had Jorie anticipated his anxiety about food? Yes, there was no other way, his unease that they would serve him bacon along with the eggs. She handed him a thick tuna sandwich on a roll. Nobody even noticed. His sense of relief was palpable. *Maybe she does understand.*

Just as they were packing up the leftovers, a couple of cows appeared out of the brush and a sound between a braying donkey and a roaring lion followed closely behind them. It wasn't hard to deduce from the bellow that it was a monster of a beast.

"Oh, oh! Get a move on everybody, the party's over," Marcel yelled. Throwing everything into a bag helter skelter they started running towards the fence laughing wildly. Jorie stumbled on the rocks and David quickly grabbed her by the arm pulling her to her feet. Scrambling over the fence rails to safety, they ran for the cars as the bull crashed through the brush behind them pulling up short at the fence.

On the drive to Jordan's place they continued laughing and joking at their near escape. Marcel stated he was confident he would have distracted the bull with his red bathing trunks and saved them all.

"Yeah Mr. Big Hero, that's why you and David got stuck trying to get through the car door at the same time," Hella piped up, which set off another bout of laughter.

Arriving at Jordan's they sat around for half an hour having a beer and then took off in his motor boat. Vicky and Ellie decided to stay behind. Before David had a chance to decline, Jorie had fastened a life jacket on him. Pulling up in the middle of the lake, Marcel vaulted over the side of the boat slipping easily into the water. Sliding the skis onto his feet, he managed to impress the crew with his athletic ability when he continued on one ski, dropping the other.

At odds with himself, David was both excited and nervous. He could never do that. He was from the city. A Yeshiva bocher - a student of the Talmud. The most country he had ever been in were the few times his father took him out of town to visit his peddling accounts.

But there was Jorie encouraging, "jump in David!"

After his hesitation at the quarry, he felt he badly needed to salvage his masculine image in her eyes.

"Marcel is going to stay in the water and show you how to get up." On impulse, his heart racing, he took a leap of faith and jumped into the bottomless water. The life-jacket kept him buoyant. Inserting his feet in the skis, Marcel handed him the tow rope and showed him the correct sitting position. Taking the ladder into the boat, he gave the signal to go. David felt the tug – his arm and leg muscles contracted and up he popped onto the water with the first try. *And I'm staying up!* It was euphoric as the water skimmed by underneath his feet — *she was right. it **is** like walking on water.* A broad grin spread across his face. Jorie was cheering him on from the back of the boat with two thumbs up.

After a couple of passes around the bay, all too soon it came to an end. Gliding to a sinking finish, he lay floating buoyantly on his back looking up at the big blue sky, the fluffy clouds and feeling the warmth of sunlight on his face. He was being reborn. *It's okay to do things out of my comfort zone. It's alright. And what crime have I committed for having 'frivolous' enjoyment?* Something was transforming David's outlook on life. For a few fleeting moments he was simply existing. No guilt, no inner voices niggling at him, just himself, his body bobbing gently on the water without a care in the world.

When the boat pulled up next to him, he had a pang of regret. He wanted that feeling of freedom to last forever, not to disappear like a burst bubble.

Later that evening, lugging their back-packs to the cars, David asked Jorie if she would like to drive home with him instead of Marcel and Hella. She eagerly accepted. On the way back to the city David reached for her hand telling her about his feeling on the skis and how he wanted to make a change in his life.

He was resigned. He was falling in love with her, and willing to bear the consequences regardless of the looming feeling of disaster for both of them.

"So David, when can I meet your family?" she asked him, direct as always. She hadn't forgotten Hella's cautionary warning — 'you'll never be accepted' — she refused to believe it. *It's impossible that they would judge me as a person based on the simple fact that I'm not Jewish.*

"We'll see."

She bristled yanking her hand away. "'We'll see'. Why the hesitation? Are you ashamed of me?"

"Of course not! You know that's not it."

"I'm not a bad person, you know." Feeling like she had to qualify that fact was making her even angrier.

"You don't have to tell me that. But," he said, reaching for her hand again, "how can I explain it. They can like you – might even really like you as a person, but not as a suitable person for marriage."

Jorie yanked her hand away. David knew it was impossible to make her understand, and for the rest of the drive home a heavy silence hung in the car. Jorie was fuming that David seemed to assume she was too dense to understand. They wouldn't think she was good enough? Why wouldn't he even give her a chance to prove herself. She was sure she could charm them into liking her.

***

After the weekend, instead of things heating up, there was a distinct coolness between them. Jorie was frustrated.

Monday while she was having lunch in the office kitchen with Hella she recounted what a great time they had had in the country and now, nothing.

"I don't understand David. He just shuts down whenever I ask him about his family. It's so frustrating. What, are they so monstrously scary a grown man lives in fear of them? You know, Mr. Abbott is really impressed with David. He says he's got a great future ahead of him, so how can a smart person let himself be ruled by other people's decisions?"

"Jorie...what do you want me to say." Hella put down her sandwich, twitching her fingers to get the crumbs off. "He's right you know. It's not going to work between you. Look, I don't know David very well, but I know the family dynamics of Jews like his parents, who escaped from Europe. They're very tight knit. No matter how good life seems in this country, there's always an underlying fear that things could erupt against them. It's a natural instinct after centuries of persecution. In it's most simplistic form, they feel their only safety is by sticking together and that definitely doesn't include their son marrying a 'shikseh'."

Momentarily distracted, "Shikseh? What's a shikseh?"

"A not so nice word for a non-Jewish girl."

"But, don't they see that by marrying someone like me, I would protect him from those very things they're afraid of?"

"In a more utopian world it would be so. But that's not reality." Hella had sympathy for her friend. She knew she was good-hearted and well-intentioned, but underneath, she had been brought up sheltered and had a naïvety about the realities of the world. Unlike me, she thought bitterly. Maybe that's why we get along so well. We're total opposites. She's like a kitten and I'm a tiger. Her thoughts drifted to Marcel. He understands me. He's definitely helped me get my shit together.

Just then, David entered the lunch room. Seeing them in the corner by the refrigerator, he walked over. "What dire plots are you two conspiring about?"

"Oh, I was just schooling our innocent little friend here on the intricacies of our tribe. Sit boychick, sit." Hella said, kicking out a chair for David.

David ran his fingers along his shirt collar. "I'd love to, but unfortunately work awaits me, unlike you two slackers," he said, taking his sandwich out of the refrigerator.

On his way out of the kitchen Mary-Ann and another girl from accounting brushed by David. "Isn't he the coolest guy?" Mary-Ann said to her friend in a dreamy voice, but loud enough for Jorie and Hella to hear.

"Yeah," Hella responded under her breath. "Cool alright, like a frozen popsicle."

Jorie was never one to let grievances fester. She preferred the head on attack and let the chips fall where they may. She couldn't focus on work wondering what David's problem was. *I know we have feelings for each other, so why does he run hot and cold. He needs to tell me what's really eating him.*
Walking down the hall to his office, *speak calmly, don't attack, be calm,* she nervously knocked on his closed door and entered, immediately blurting out, "David, can we go somewhere after work to talk? You've been avoiding me since we were in the country. I thought we had such a good time and then suddenly nothing."

"What about?" he said.

"What about what?" Jorie asked confused.

"What is there to talk about?"
Ooo, he is maddening. She hadn't intended to get into something heavy right here in the office.

"Well, you must have some idea of what I want to talk about. Don't you? Or are you just playing dumb to avoid things you don't want to face?"

"What do you want from me, Jorie?" he said, annoyingly in a too calm voice.
Oh, this is too much! He's being deliberately obtuse. "I want to know where we stand! You can't pretend there's nothing

between us - you seem to want me and then all of a sudden you pull back; for no reason I can think of. Maybe you'd like to enlighten me?"

"Alright, but now is not -" Before he could continue, the intercom buzzed. Answering it, he said, "right away," and hung up. "You'll have to excuse me. Mr. Abbott wants me to meet a new account in his office."

"But what about…"

"We'll get together later."

"When later?"

"Soon." And with that he jumped up and walked by her striding down the hall.

Oooo, he's so infuriating! What's his problem anyway? She stalked out of his office and down the hallway to her desk. Her heart was beating a-mile-a-minute. Well, so much for staying calm, she berated herself. There was a post-it phone message on her blotter, the fifth one from Jace. He had been calling her persistently since his uninvited intrusion at Duck Lake. *The man has no shame when it comes to something he's on the hunt for.*

Thinking about it for a few minutes she decided to return his call. Mitch was also in town and wanted to see her. Maybe it was time to go out with somebody who wasn't into playing games. Or, if they were, she didn't care, because she only wanted David. But they would at least be a distraction and screw David, she said to herself.

Chapter Thirteen

Jace wheeled into the office parking lot. Leaning over, he opened the passenger door. Shielding her hair from the rain with a newspaper, she stepped from under the portico and jumped into the front seat. He looked great – freshly shaved and showered, dressed to kill, he had obviously gone to some trouble putting himself together for her. They were going to have dinner and go to a movie afterword. He was giving her all his attention. She understood that the chase was on again.

"I'm so glad you were free this evening," he said, reaching for her hand and caressing it with his thumb. It was amazing how she used to melt at his touch and now it didn't do a thing for her. She just wanted to have a good time and take her mind off David.

They drove across town towards the restaurant in silence. Used to be when they were together, she always asked about his day and how things were going for him. Her life had revolved around his needs and wants and she felt as though she always had to keep his interest. Suddenly she found herself totally detached and was quite happy not having to think about fulfilling his needs or agonize about what he was doing when he wasn't with her. It was a big relief and she was pleased to recognize that feeling. She seldom stopped to think about what she wanted or what she was doing with her life. She more or less just went blundering along with the flow leaving decisions to whatever was going on at the moment.

"You're very quiet. I thought you'd have more to say since we haven't seen each other for some time."

"I'm just thinking."

"Hah, now that's a first."

She snatched her hand away and pulled in her chin. "What are you implying? That I'm simple minded?"

"Don't be so sensitive. Just that you're usually very spontaneous and a chatter-box. I'm not used to pensive Jorie."

"I have things on my mind."

"You're not thinking of that guy I saw you with at the lake are you?"

Like I'm going to tell you, she thought with a hhmph.

They pulled up in the parking lot of the restaurant.

Jace put the car in park and turned to her. "He's not your type Jorie. You know that, don't you?"

"What's my type, Jace? Someone who cheats on me and takes me for granted?"

"C'mon, you're not going to start that?"

"I'm asking you. What's my type?" she snapped.

Disgruntled, Jace replied, "never mind, let's just have a nice dinner and catch up with each other."

Her head pressed against the car window; she had a sudden impulse that she wanted to go back to her apartment. It didn't matter that now she had the upper hand. She wasn't like a predatory, self-serving male hoping to turn a bad situation to her advantage. She didn't care and with that, the realization hit her that she and Jace couldn't even be friends. He wasn't a straight shooter – he would never see a woman as a true friend, only as prey. Tears suddenly welled in her eyes. Was there even such a thing as a happy relationship? Or were they all battles to be fought and won and fought again.

Swallowing and with a big sigh, she asked, "Why did you want to see me, Jace?"

"What do you mean, why? Because I care about you and I thought we had something special, that's why."

"But what's changed between me and you? Were you seeing someone after we spilt and now I'm a convenient stop-over? I want to go home."

"What, now?"

"Yes, now. Please!"

"But we didn't even..."

"Please!"

"You are really a piece of work Jorie. I don't know what's happened to you."

Once Jorie would have tried to justify herself, but now, she realized, she just wanted to be rid of him.

Looking down at the parking lot through the rain spattered window David saw the flashy sports car pull in. Jorie raced out from under the portico holding a something over her hair. *So, he's still in the picture. Well, why shouldn't he be. I have nothing to offer her. Why do I feel so angry then? I have to move out, find my own place. Adam has his own life now. Ruth is engaged and will always be critical no matter what I do.*

Picking up the phone he dialed his older brother's house. "Adam, can I stop by your place after work?"

"Plan on dinner. I'll let Rachel know you're coming."
Parking at the rear of the house, Adam was chopping vegetables in the kitchen when David came through the back door. The smell of frying onions made his mouth water. Automatically his hand went to the mezuzah on the door jamb. The main floor duplex was clean, the nondescript furniture dull and old-fashioned, but neatly dispersed throughout the large rooms.

Rachel greeted David warmly. A blonde with a natural high flush on her cheeks, pretty in a wholesome way, but quiet and serious – unlike Jorie, David thought, angry at himself that he would compare Rachel with Jorie. Two different worlds. Adam's marriage had been arranged and he and Rachel had only met briefly before the ceremony, but they both seemed to be content with the resulting union. Rachel was already pregnant.

"You boys go sit in the living room. I'll finish getting dinner ready."

The perfect 'baleboosteh' – a perfect housekeeper, David thought as he walked across the green wall to wall carpeting and sat on the end of the sofa. *Why couldn't I be happy with that?* Adam took the other corner.

"So little brother mine, what brings you to our neck of the neighborhood tonight?" Adam had an easy going way about him. Nothing ever seemed to ruffle his feathers. *Maybe because he does everything right. Why do I always have to be the shit-stirrer and he's always Mr. Perfect?"*

"I need some advice and NOT any judgement, alright?"

"Sounds serious. Go ahead. I'll do my best."

"I've met a girl…"

"Let me guess. She's not Jewish."

David shuffled his feet and looked down at the pea green carpet. "I can't explain the attraction between us Adam. She's so different, full of energy and life and she laughs and has fun…and, she has a horse. We went riding together. Her parents seem to like me. They don't care that I'm Jewish…" he was babbling, trying way too hard to convince Adam. Adam held up his hand.

"David, what do you want me to tell you? If it was just me, I would say, go for it – although from how you're describing her, I can't see her fitting in with our family. But you know all too well the consequences of your actions. Is it fair to her? She'll always be an outsider. Ruth will never accept her and for sure the Pa won't and what about friends and family functions?"

"Ruth is a high strung judgmental bitch," David said, his pent up anger making him feel bitter.

"C'mon David. That's a little harsh. High strung, yes, but not a bitch. She's always been concerned about the Pa and Ma. How deep are you in with this girl?"

"I've been holding her at arm's length, trying to reason myself out of caring about her but if I keep doing it, I'm afraid I'm going to lose her."

"And…nu? So? You will get over her you know."

"But why do I have to 'get over her', live my life by the dictates of other people? If I told them to live their life a certain way, would they obey me?"

"Have you mentioned the possibility of conversion to her?"

"We aren't at that stage, besides, she has some pretty strong negative opinions about religions…"

Adam looked at David with sympathy. He knew it had never been easy for his younger brother to stay within the lines. But he also knew the consequences if he gave him the approval he was looking for.

"How well do you really know her and her family that you would be willing to give up your own family, because you know that's what's going to happen…I mean, Ma might…but the Pa, I don't have to spell it out and what if you become serious with her and all of a sudden her parents aren't thrilled about you anymore."

David couldn't even entertain the point Adam was making.

"I want to be free, Adam! Don't you understand? I'm only getting this one trip to Earth and I want to be free to explore – without guilt – without being held responsible for my family's feelings. Hell, do they feel guilty for inhibiting me?" David raked his fingers through his thick dark hair and tugged on his shirt collar. After a pause, he started again. "Maybe sometimes relationships just don't fit within the confines of other's expectations. I know what our parents went through. But that's their story. What about my story? Don't I get a chance to have my own?"

"Okay boychick, calm down." Adam said, moving closer and putting his hand on David's shoulder.

"I need to be alone," David said, shrugging off Adam's hand, jumping up from the sofa and striding to the front door. "Tell Rachel I'm sorry I couldn't stay."

***

After a huffy goodbye from Jace, back in her apartment she took a Tylenol for the impending headache and lay down on her bed feeling sorry for herself. *I need to get a cat. Even if my parents let me borrow Catdog, he can't stay home all day alone while I go to work. A nice big fat cat that would lie on my stomach and purr. Men are so stupid.*

The doorbell rang. *Maybe it's Hella; no, she would have called first. Ignore it. It better not be Jace.* It rang again and again. Maybe the damn building is on fire, she muttered to herself getting off the bed and stomping down the hallway.

Angrily, she threw open the door.

"David! What are you doing here?"

"Can I come in or do you have company?"

"I'm alone. Come in," she said, stepping aside to let him through.

"I thought maybe your friend, Jace, was here." David could barely say his name without gritting his teeth.

"Oh, him. No. As you can see, I'm all by my lonesome."

She led him into the living room. He had not been to her apartment since he helped her move.

"The place looks great."

"Thank you. That's why you came by, to check out what I've done with it?"

David winced at the sarcasm in her voice.

131

"No, actually, I came by to talk to you, seriously."

"Okay, I'm ready. Let's go." She walked over and chose the single chair so he couldn't sit next to her.

Her cavalier attitude threw him. "Jorie, please. This isn't easy for me."

"David, what can be so terrible that you have to be so dramatic."

"Damn it! I'm not being dramatic. I'm serious."

She had never seen him lose his temper. "I apologize. I was in a bad mood before you got here. I'm sorry, please tell me what it is. Would you like something to drink first? Are you hungry?"

He shook his head. He had his speech planned on the drive over and now it was all falling apart. He didn't know where to start so he blurted out, "you know how you asked when you could meet my family?" Jorie nodded. "Well, you can't. Probably never."

This was nowhere near what she expected to hear from him.

"Not because of you," he added hastily, seeing her stunned expression. "Because of them." His hand went to the neck of his shirt.

He tried to explain how he would be ostracized if they knew about her and how they would have to live a double life if they wanted to be together. "Do you understand what ostracization means?" He could tell from the questioning look on her face that she understood the word but was positive she didn't understand the full force of what it entailed.

"I'll be an outcast. People from the neighborhood I've known all my life will cross the street to avoid me. My father for sure will forbid Adam and Ruth and worse, my mother, from talking to me. It will be as if I'm a nonperson to everyone and everything I've known all my life."

"David, I...I don't know what to say. I can't even imagine...because of me? Someone they don't even know?"

"I'm looking for a place of my own. That will solve part of the problem. My parents are elderly, not young and modern like yours, and I don't want to cause them more grief. Do you think you can live that kind of life?"

"David," she was trying to digest a concept she never imagined, shaking her head, "I'll have to think about the whole thing. So does that mean we could never get married? You want us to live together? I mean, marriage certainly hasn't been a priority on my list, but to be forced not to, because of people I can't even meet? That's not logical is it?"

"I don't know...unless you would consider converting?"

"Can't you just accept me as I am? I'm not asking you to give up your religion."

Jorie was perplexed. She loved David, but this was a whole other life-changing bunch of information to think about.

"I know it seems complicated, but we can make it work and I promise you, things will get better. Please come and sit beside me," he said, reaching out his hand towards her.

Reluctantly, she sat down next to him. He turned her head towards him and kissed her. One of those dreamy, soft pillow kisses, that sent her out of reality. But she wanted more from him. She wanted to possess him – to show him how it feels so that he would never forget and maybe then he would change his mind and want her more than all the complications he had laid out. Suddenly an urgency overtook them. She led him into her bedroom.

"Is this your first time David?" thinking back that he had never mentioned if his marriage was consummated or not. Not answering, he let his hands and his mouth speak for him.

Afterward they lay there entwined in each others arms, his leg over hers and just held each other until Jorie wriggled lose and leaned up on one elbow and looked down into his dark sleepy eyes, her teeth covering her bottom lip in puzzlement. "David," she said while twisting the dark hair on his chest into curls around her finger, " I'm not going to ask again, but if this was your first time, I think you have an innate talent you've been keeping secret."

"Oh my god Jorie…shut up and lie down here," he said, a small contented smile on his lips as he pulled her head back down to his shoulder.

"Why are you so embarrassed when I compliment you?" her voice muffled in his shoulder. She tried to sit back up but he tightened his grip.

"Shhh…I'm not embarrassed…it's just that…sometimes things don't need to be said. They just are. You always have a need to examine and psychoanalyze everything."

"Rather than sweeping everything under the carpet, you mean – until there's a big lump of crap that's too heavy to get rid of?"

David exhaled a loud sigh. "What do you want me to say?"

"I want you to say what you think, what you feel, what I mean to you – how it's going to work between us."

"Alright, let me sleep a little while and I promise we'll talk when I get up."

He was already beginning to nod off. She listened to his steady breathing and lay there thinking. *Men are so simplistic. Feed me, screw me, let me avoid what I don't want to deal with and just be happy and nice. Aagh. So what am I going to get out of this? Why am I being asked to make all the sacrifices? But I love him.*

She closed her eyes and dozed awhile until eventually, nature called and Jorie reluctantly left the warmth of his body and the bed.

David felt her stir and began to wake up. Slipping a t-shirt over her head, Jorie exclaimed, "I'm starving! Tomato soup, crackers and cheese – sound good?"

"Very good." He reached out pulling her back onto the bed. "I love you Jorie, Miss Jorie-Anne Fielding," he said, softly curling himself around her.

"You do? Well I'm happy to hear it because the feeling is mutual "

***

David had a new attitude – they agreed that they should keep their romance out of the office gossip mill. Of course Jorie told Hella because she knew Hella would die before she would spill a secret and she needed someone to share her excitement with.

After going back and forth, a month later they agreed to move into David's apartment. It was larger than Jorie's and closer to work. Her parents weren't overjoyed about the living together, and of course David hadn't told his family, but Jorie was convinced that things would change when she and David had a solid relationship between them and if she was honest with herself, marriage had never been something she yearned for. Bride dolls, when she was a kid, had never been her thing. Ranches and horses, that was her passion.

It wasn't long before a darker side of David began to emerge. There was a deep well of guilt within him that Jorie couldn't reach no matter how hard she tried. The very personality traits that had drawn them together, her spontaneity, her childlike enthusiasm of ordinary events seemed to be the things that grated most on him. She found him over-sensitive – about his own feelings, not hers. She couldn't cook the Jewish food he had grown up with. There were a whole new set of rules she learned that had to be followed or David became unglued. She sometimes forgot not to mix meat and dairy products – a normal thing in her 'before' world. His harsh criticism of her inattention left her stunned and shamed – she began to feel like a failure. David was either calm and controlled or would explode like a firecracker. Standing over her and yelling insults, she began to feel that he was crushing her spirit. And it didn't matter how hard she strived to make things right, it was never the correct thing.

The apartment kitchen was small and she set the limit – the kitchen didn't have room for two sets of dishes, cutlery, pots and pans – even if she had wanted to keep kosher, which she didn't. She reasoned that way back when people didn't have modern washing facilities, it was probably safer, but now with soap and hot water…No, she just wouldn't do it.

She began to think that he was trying to have her recreate his mother's home. He said he wanted to be free, but his actions were saying something else and she wondered if his upbringing had left an indelible mark on his brain that he would never be free of.

And of course, there were family functions, to which she was excluded.

Jorie found herself with lots of time on her hands, but the day he got all dressed up to go to Ruth's wedding, alone, reality suddenly took on a whole new dimension.

She was watching him put on his black tuxedo. "My gosh, you look so handsome, David," she said, standing back and admiring him.

His sister had managed to snag a lawyer who was paying the tab for an extravagant wedding. When David came home later that evening, Jorie was excited to hear all about it, but he avoided her questions. She was hurt and the reality that something in the relationship was unbalanced hit her like a sledge-hammer.

It hadn't happened overnight. It crept up on her like a thief in the dark, stealing her sense of self, her personality, her spirit. When they were alone together or with friends, they had fun, but she came to realize there were two David's. Jorie had half and even that half was divided into a quarter good and a quarter bad and his family had the other half. *Am I willing to settle for half a person?*

The holiday of Passover was spent at his parents. Jorie stayed home, soaking in a long hot bath, eating a tuna sandwich on crumbly matzo instead of the squishy fresh white bread she liked , running the hot water tap with her toes as the water cooled and reading a trashy tabloid. It used to be one of her favorite treats, but now it seemed somehow like the consolation prize.

On Friday nights, it was routine for David to go to Adam's house for Shabbos dinner. If Jorie wanted to go out somewhere with friends, there would be a scene. Never about the actual problem, but David would find something to criticize her for and storm out, leaving her shaken. His temper tantrums became more and more frequent. Jorie had come to believe that she was the source of all their problems even though she tried her best to be what he wanted. She understood from reading that anger was a cover-up for deep fear – but still, she had to save herself before she could hope to save him or their relationship.

When Rosh Hashanah and Yom Kippur came around and he informed her he was staying at his parents because 'it's forbidden to drive', Jorie could see he would never be free. The umbilical cord of religious indoctrination was too strong.

Little by little she felt herself slipping away. She constantly berated herself for being the source of David's anger. After a particularly nasty weekend she was taking a bath and thought that if she just turned face-down and drowned, the pain would go away. This thought had started to permeate her mind.

She found it increasingly difficult to work in the same office when David carried over his anger and sulking towards her.

Leave him, she told herself over and over, but her weakness was empathy. Looking at him sleeping with his troubled brow scrunched between his eyes and remembering the stories about his father beating him when he was young, she would feel his pain. Reasoning with herself that rather than confronting his father about the humiliation, he choked it down until it was a rage, hot and explosive. And yet, she hated herself for being the weak one.

And then just like storm clouds clearing out of the sky, the anger would disappear. They went places; they had fun together – he told her he loved her. Away from his family, he relaxed and let down his guard. But the underlying tension was never far away. They had to be back for Shabbos. He never travelled on a Friday night or Saturday – he couldn't do that. If they went somewhere by car, he would begin getting tense on the drive home to make sure he was at Adam's for Shabbos dinner. They would fight in the car. He was obsessed. No stopping for lunch or sightseeing; just drive, drive, until he felt he was safely home before sunset Friday.

It was beyond Jorie how to deal with it. It wasn't hard to figure out that guilt was eating him up. This was the person she wanted to see laugh and instead, she was becoming like the person he was when they first met, unable to experience joy and laughter anymore. It had crept in and eaten away at her until she would look in the mirror and wonder who she was, who is this husk of a mentally beaten and braindead person staring back at her. She used to be fun and vibrant. Maybe she was too frivolous, too superficial, as David often told her, but wasn't that why he had fallen in love with her. Because she brought some levity into his stolid life? She didn't know. She had lost confidence in her ability to see things clearly.

As much as she tried reasoning with him, explaining why she thought he had so much anger, nothing worked. Anger, fear and guilt – it was a lethal combination and she seemed helpless to extricate herself from the mire.

Then abruptly everything changed.

Chapter Fourteen

"My father's been shot!" David exclaimed. "I have to go to the hospital." He came barreling out of his office and down the hallway. The blood drained from his face.

"What? Wait," Jorie said, running to get her coat. "I'll go with you."

"No, you can't come. You stay here."

"But David..."

"Go home after work. I'll call you."

Crestfallen, Jorie sat back down at her desk. It suddenly exploded in her brain that she was the person in the closet – the big secret – the pariah – the outcast.

Hella came through the walnut doors and wanted to know why David had flew by them in such a panic. Jorie told her what happened.

"Hella, I can't just stay here at work. He needs me. I should be there with him – can you come to the hospital with me? He was so distraught, he probably wasn't thinking right when he rushed out."

"I'll go with you, but I don't think it's in your best interests to be there at this time."

And besides she had seen the price Jorie was already paying for being with David and had grown none too fond of him at this point.

Driving across town she tried to prepare Jorie for what she could expect if other family members were there. But Jorie was too preoccupied with comforting David to ingest it.

Arriving at the hospital, they wound their way through the corridors until they came to the emergency ward. In the waiting room Jorie spotted an elderly gray-haired woman with reddened eyes sitting next to a dark haired woman in her late twenties, her obvious wig pulled back into a severe pony tail, but no David. She must be David's sister, Ruth, Jorie thought. The woman was staring at her with narrowed eyes.

"Excuse me, is this where Mr. Kaisman is?" Jorie asked the younger woman.

"Who are you?" came a cold question.

"Ah... I'm a, a friend of David's." Hella was standing in the background quietly observing the situation.

"Please LEAVE."

"I'm sorry?" Jorie's eyelids fluttered and color rose into her face.

"LEAVE! Can't you see we don't want you here?" Her eyes had narrowed to slits.

Hella stepped forward as if to shield Jorie. "Hey, hold on a minute there girlie...I understand you're distraught but..."

"Who are *you*?" Ruth stood up. Her face was black with fury.

"I'm, we, are both friends of David's if you don't mind. In fact, she," indicating Jorie, "is a very close friend and..."

"I know who SHE is," Ruth spat in fury. "Get out of here. You're ruining my brother! You're killing our family, kurveh!" Ruth screeched.

"Slut! Who are you calling a slut? How dare you! My friend is no slut, you bitch," Hella exclaimed.

Jorie was stunned at the back and forth. Beyond mortified. She was about to run off when Adam came bustling out of his father's room.

"What's all the commotion out here?"

Looking quickly at the faces, he sized up the problem. Going to his sister he held his hand up. "Ruth, calm down. You're causing a disturbance. If these people are friends of David's, let him speak to them when he comes out. Now is not the time." He gently pushed a fuming Ruth back onto her chair. David's mother sat there passively watching the unfolding scene.

"I don't want HER here," Ruth said, through clenched teeth.

This was beyond anything Jorie had ever experienced. Tears sprang to her eyes. She wanted to run out of the hospital or disappear into the floor.

Hella took her by the arm. "Adam is it?" Adam nodded. "We'll go to the cafeteria for coffee. When David comes out, he can meet us there, if he cares to. We're sorry about your father," she finished, barely able to contain her seething anger.

Hella paid for the coffee and placed the two cups on the cafeteria table. Jorie's hand shook as she reached for her cup.

"What just happened? I never imagined..."

"I tried to warn you Jor Jor. If there's a fanatic in the family...this was not exactly the best time to introduce yourself," she said with an impish smile, raising her eyebrows.

"I was sure at least he told them something. We've been together for months. How could he keep our relationship, me, such a secret?"

"Uh, in case you didn't notice, you're not that much of a secret, and easy, he's trying to keep the peace at the expense of... Brace yourself, here he comes."

David zeroed in on the two of them sitting at a rear table. His face told them what to expect.

"Jorie, I thought I told you not to come here."

"But your father…I wanted to be here for you."

"Well, you saw how it upset my family, and they certainly didn't need that."

"Hey! Wait just a minute David," Hella jumped to Jorie's defense. "'Normal people' don't understand the mentality of fundamentalism. It's your own fault for being too weak to face the music and keeping Jorie 'in the closet'."

Flustered, David turned to Jorie, "please stay here if you must. I don't think my father has long to live and I may be in the emergency for a while. We'll talk when I get home."

After David left, Hella saw the toll it had taken on Jorie. "Why don't you pick up some clothes and spend the night at my place. Who knows what time David will be home and what mood he'll be in – you're not going to be able to sleep as it is."

"But if his father dies.."

"You can't do anything. They'll shut you out. You saw how hysterical that bitch was. Besides, if he does die, they have funeral arrangements to make. He has to be buried within twenty-four hours."

"So is this the way it's always going to be? He'll always live two lives?"

"Unless he gets the balls to choose – sadly, that's what you have to look forward to. Although I have to say, while 'sweet little Ruthie' was carrying on the attack, his mother didn't say a thing. Maybe if she loves him as much as you always said, she might come around after the old man is gone. God! I hate religious dictators!" Hella said, slamming her cup down on the table.

***

Emotionally drained, David turned the key in the apartment door. It was 3:30 Sunday morning. He felt sick to his stomach over the way he behaved with Jorie.

Stepping inside, he hoped Jorie wouldn't be…he didn't know what to expect. She had a right to be upset, but he was too exhausted to answer any questions. And he knew she would have questions – about their relationship. Quietly, hoping she was asleep, he checked the bedroom. The bed hadn't been slept in. The closet door was open and he saw her overnight bag was gone. Panic spread through him. *She's gone. She's left me.* That was all he needed. He lay down on the bed fully clothed. The events of the day suddenly all became a reality.

David had just succumbed to the netherworld of half sleep and wakefulness when the doorbell jolted him fully awake. *It's Jorie – she forgot her keys.* He glanced at the clock on the dresser. 4:40 AM. Wearily he dragged his body off the bed and opened the door. Two policemen were standing there.

"Mr. Kaisman? We're sorry to intrude at this time of the morning, please accept our condolences. It's imperative that we start the investigation as quickly as possible." They took in his reddened eyes and disheveled appearance. "We have to ask you a few questions. Your father was murdered and we'd like to know if you have any idea why or who might have had a grudge against him. Can we come in? We'll try to be brief."

After explaining about the pawn shop robbery and the man his father crippled during the fight, so long ago, the police officers left. They remarked that criminals and their families have long memories and assured him they would do everything they could to catch the murderer.

Going back to his bed, he lay down, folded his arms behind his head and stared at the ceiling fixture dozing. Dawn was starting to filter in through the blinds.

The phone rang startling him. He must have slept. He checked his watch. Eight-thirty. It was Adam. "We're going to the funeral home to make the arrangements. Are you coming?"

"I think Jorie left me."

"Left you? I'm sure she didn't, but let's deal with this first. Can you pull yourself together?"

"I don't know. *I think I'm falling apart.* I have to call the office."

"It's Sunday. Stay home. Get some sleep. I'll call you when we're finished."

A pounding headache; he lay back down bunching the pillow under his head. A chain of dis-jointed thoughts began floating and expanding in his mind. *Adam the calm one, the good one. Easy for him. He always does the right thing. Ruth, the Pa's favorite. Me, the big screw-up. Why couldn't I just conform? Go along with the program. Make life easier on myself. But I haven't done either. She's right to leave me. Was I trying not to cause my parents grief, or myself, or just not strong enough to face the consequences? Or was it fear of the Pa's contempt. Well, one part of that is solved.*

Every muscle in his body was strung tight – he felt rigid as a board. Head pounding like his skull bone was being hit by a hammer. *The Pa is dead. Jorie has left me. The Pa is dead. Jorie has left me. The Pa is dead. Jorie has...* He dozed off into a fitful sleep.

***

At 9:30 AM the apartment door opened. Jorie stood in the bedroom looking at a sleeping David curled in a fetal position, his face troubled even in sleep, still dressed in yesterday's rumpled clothes. Her heart broke to see him in such misery, looking so vulnerable, but still, it was his choice, not hers. *Stay strong,* she heard Hella's voice. If he wouldn't take her into his world, she couldn't force him. The sting of his sister Ruth's spiteful words still rang in her head. It was difficult to believe that someone who didn't know her, could hate her so much. Even though Hella explained that she shouldn't take it personally – it didn't matter who the girl was, if she wasn't Jewish, it would have been the same. It was beyond her comprehension – but it brought clarity to the whole situation and what she had to do.

David stirred and opened bleary eyes. "You've come back. I thought you left me."

"David I've decided…" She mustn't let herself get caught up in feeling sorry for him.

"My father died." He said simply.

All her restraint disappeared. "Oh David, I'm so sorry." She was sorry, but if she was honest, she couldn't feel much sympathy for the man who had never been a kind father to David and had raised a daughter full of hate and fear. She sat down on the side of the bed even though it was a mistake, if she touched him, she was sure she would come undone. She reached out and rubbed his back.

"The funeral is today."

The words hung in the air like a thunder cloud. She knew the answer before she asked the question but she couldn't stop herself.

"Do you want me to come with you?"

David turned toward the wall. That was her answer.

Completely crushed, she got up, packed the rest of her things and left the apartment.

Chapter Fifteen

After the cemetery, everyone was invited back to Ruth's house. Plentiful hot and cold food had been sent in by friends and neighbors, and along with a bowl of hard boiled eggs, an assortment of kosher cold cuts, breads, pickles, coleslaw and pastries were already gracing a table set up in the large kitchen. A pitcher of water and a basin were placed on a chair outside the front door to wash your hands and in effect, wash away the spiritual impurity of the cemetery. The mirrors were covered to ensure that mourners were unconcerned about personal appearance – ties were rent to express the pain and sorrow of the passing and to represent the tear in the mourner's heart. The low chairs had been set up in the living room where the family would spend the next seven days, sitting Shiva for the Pa and greeting mourners.

David went through the motions in a trance. *Who is that person? That weak person sitting on the little chair. That person wants to stand up and scream! I don't want to carry all my family's pain and sorrow on my back anymore. I want to be free! The Pa is gone. My judge, my condemner is gone. How bad am I to think of him like that. He did his best. And I always let him down.* But if he was honest with himself, wasn't he just a tiny bit relieved that the Pa was dead? *I loved him. I hated him. I am the one undeserving of love. Look at me – the Pa is dead – and I'm filled with these self-pitying thoughts.* Shaking hands and accepting condolences.

There was a tension welling up so strongly, he felt his insides were twisting into a painful, life-threatening knot. He was afraid if he could no longer restrain himself, he would be committed to a hospital. He had heard of religious Jews having nervous breakdowns and being committed to a psychiatric ward.

Jumping up, he excused himself and rushed outside for some fresh air. He noted a police car parked at the end of the block. Watching for the murderer. *People on their way in shake my hand, offering condolences. They only see my outside and I think I'm behaving well.* Searching the street hoping to see Jorie, maybe sitting in the car watching for him, being there for him, if not able to be next to him. *Whose fault is that? MINE! THEIRS! ALL OF US! ALL OF US WHO MAKE US PAY FOR WHAT WE DIDN'T DO. THEY WANT CONTROL OF ME. I WANT CONTROL OF ME. What am I thinking? I'm going crazy. Walk.*
He was having an anxiety attack. His organs were vibrating and he could hear a loud thumping like a drum – it was his heart. *What if she really left me. The Pa is dead. He's still beating me. Why am I thinking about her? I'm betraying his memory. He's dead and now I can be free. But there's Ruth and Adam and my mother. The neighbors…Everyone's watching me. I'm letting everyone down.*

A hand on his shoulder startled him. "Want to come back in little brother? Everything okay? Ma is concerned about you."

How could he explain. David's face reddened and he burst out. "Adam, I don't know who I am? I'm not a good son. I've never been. You were always the good one. And now? He's gone and look what I did to him? I let him down. I've let everybody down. Even myself." Tears ran down his face in streaks. Adam took a handkerchief from his pocket and handed it to David. He

148

had never seen his younger brother like this before. The beatings his father had given him, the humiliation, David had seemed to brush it all off.

People coming up the sidewalk to the house still insisted on shaking hands with them. *Can't they see?* David wanted to scream at them, *CAN'T YOU SEE? I AM NOBODY. I'M A PUPPET! A PATHETIC PUPPET WITHOUT A MIND. Centuries of people are pulling my strings and now I'm limp. I've fallen. I'm without a puppeteer. A Yeshiva bocher puppet.* Guilt was crushing him like some medieval torture he had read about. A huge stone was on his chest and he couldn't breathe. He gasped for breath and shuddered.

"David, listen to me." Adam led him to the side of the building and looked straight into his face. "I know what this is all about and I'm going to help you. Let's just get through the Shiva and we'll talk. Alright? Come back to the house. I'll make your excuses and you'll go into a bedroom and lie down. Get some rest."

David started to sob, racking sobs. A dam had been unleashed. But what was he crying about? The Pa or himself? Everyone was staring. Judging. It was all he could do to follow Adam back to the house. "Here," he said, leading David into Ruth's guest room. "Take one of Ruth's sleeping pills and try and relax. Sleep. You'll feel better." Adam pulled the window drapes shut and closed the door.

David laid there. *Look how weak I am, how bad I am. I can't even sit Shiva for the Pa. The Pa never liked me. Adam and Ruth were the favorites. They lived the right way. The only way. The Pa's way.* He felt himself floating off to that place between wakefulness and sleep. It was a blessing.

A shard of morning light pierced his eyes. Disorientated he lay there focusing on a framed photo of Rabbi Schneerson on the patterned wall paper. Sounds and smells came from beyond the closed door. He remembered. Adam had put him to bed in Ruth's guest room. *What time is it?* He glanced at his watch. *Have to call the office. Get back to my apartment and take a shower. Maybe Jorie...? I have a lot to make up for.* But first he had to face Ruth and her smug lawyer husband, Irv.

"So David, you're feeling better?" Ruth asked, as David entered the kitchen. Irv nodded, barely glancing up from his newspaper.

"Yes, thanks for the bed. I have to go home and shower. I'll see you later."

"David, before you go; that girl at the hospital. She shouldn't come..."

"Ruth," Irv interrupted, not looking up from his paper. "Mind your business. It's not the time."

He couldn't wait to get out of her house. She was always a judgmental bitch he thought to himself, and then felt guilty for thinking of his sister that way. Guilt piled on top of guilt. How many pounds did guilt weigh? Nothing; but the weight of nothing was crushing him.

The apartment was empty. He knew it would be, but still... Jorie would be at the office. I'll call her and apologize.

As he went to pick up the receiver, it rang.

"David?" It was Adam. "I called Ruth's and she said you left. Everything okay? You slept well?"

"I'm okay. Sorry about yesterday."

"As long as you're feeling better." David could hear the concern in Adam's voice and felt guilty for being a burden instead of a support for Adam. "So we'll see you at Ruth's this afternoon?"

After he hung up, he noticed the flashing message light. It was Jorie.

"Hi David. Just wanted to let you know that I spoke to Mr. Abbott and told him you can't make it in this week. He was sorry to hear about your Dad and so am I..." there was a hesitancy, "I'm sorry about your dad," she said quickly and hung up.

***

David sat on the low chair in Ruth's living room going through the motions, shaking hands, allowing hugs, giving a thin smile on cue. He saw Marcel walk in and give his condolences to the family before he came to David.

"How you doin' there big guy?" he said, shaking David's hand warmly.

David felt his eyes start to pool.

"Want to get some fresh air?"

David nodded getting up. They walked together to the corner, turned around and retraced their steps.

"I can't presume to know what you're going through, my friend, but do you remember, we were raised the same and I went through something similar not so long ago."

David nodded slowly. Since they had rekindled their friendship, David just assumed Marcel was now the modern care-free person he appeared to be. He had forgotten how similar their backgrounds were.

"It wasn't easy for me either – it sounds like a cliché, but things really do get easier with time. My parents had a shit-fit when I told them I wanted to live a different life than they did. I was ostracized from the family and a lot of the friends we grew up with turned their backs on me. It was a really bad time. But look, here I am today, I survived and I have to say, I made the right decision for me. My family eventually accepted me back, but in a different way. I know what you're thinking, 'but Hella is Jewish and Jorie is not.' Only by chance, not by choice. Everyone has hard decisions to make in life and there's usually a price to pay. Ultimately 'they' don't live their lives to suit your rules.

David took a deep breath. "I know what you're saying is all true but…"

"Jorie's a nice girl David. Talk to her. I'm sure you can both come to an understanding. Hella says she really cares for you."

***

Day seven was the last day of Shiva – David likened it to sinking in quicksand and he couldn't wait for it to be over so he could pull himself out of the quagmire. No word from Jorie – he wanted to give her a call, but was afraid of what he might hear. Afraid…he was always 'afraid'. Afraid to offend his sister, Adam, the community. He thought about words he had read recently by Hillel, the great Jewish sage and scholar. 'If I am not for myself, who will be for me?'

***

Jorie had cried her last tear. She had to face the situation and get past it. She didn't want to be the girl in the closet, always taking second place to his family. She was losing what was left of herself and she couldn't go on living at Hella's forever. She had to find her own place and start over again.

Marcel had dropped by Hella's apartment that evening and was telling them about his visit with David at the Shiva house and how he was worried David was having a nervous breakdown.

Hella scoffed. "He should only grow a pair." She took a swallow of her gin and tonic. She knew she was prone to making snap judgments and regretting it later but really… "if he had to go through some of the things I went through, he'd have a real reason to have a breakdown. I never told you about my life growing up."

Marcel moved closer and put his arm around her shoulders. She was angry and shook him off. "You want to know what control is, and evil? I'll tell you what it is and then I never want to talk about it again." Jorie and Marcel didn't dare breath.

"I never knew my real sperm-donor," she said, her voice brittle, "only my step-father. Shortly after my Mum and Jake," her lip curled at the mention of his name, "married, he started using her like a punching bag. When she was pregnant with my step-brother, he punched her in the stomach trying to cause a mis-carriage. Once when I was eleven, he hit her in the face with his fist so hard she hit her head on the edge of the kitchen counter and passed out. I thought she was dead. My brother was two years old at the time. We were both crying and hugging her and Fucking Jake as I always called him, grabbed me, took me into another room and told me to undress – while my mother was lying on the kitchen floor!" Hella choked. "I tried to run out of the room but he was a hulking monster and I was no match. He tore my pajamas off and told me to get down on my hands and knees and kiss his feet because he was the one who made the money and put bread on the table. After my mother recovered, she was never the same. I think she sustained a brain injury – but what could I do? I was just a kid. A very frightened kid.

Two months later she died unexpectedly. I know he murdered her but...my aunt and uncle took my baby brother to raise and left me with Jake. After that, it was a nightmare. I was never allowed to have clothes on when he was home. He would humiliate me in every way imaginable. Pinching and probing and forcing me... I became someone else – Helen was gone, as if I lived outside my body where he couldn't touch me. I became Hella. This went on until I was fifteen. One night when he came home drunk, I stabbed him with a butcher knife. The fucker didn't even die, but I was taken and put into a foster home until my other aunt took me in. She at least had the sense to get me a good psychiatrist and after several years of therapy, voila, here I am." Her cavalier words didn't match the pain on her face.

She took a long slug from her glass. Silent tears ran down her cheeks. Marcel and Jorie looked at each other incredulously and went to hug her. "Don't! Don't feel sorry for me," she snapped.

"We don't feel sorry for you Hella, Marcel said, "we just love you."

"Why didn't you tell anyone? A teacher or a friend?"

"Let's put it this way. When someone smashes a glass bottle at the breakfast table, puts the jagged edge to your face and says he'll carve you up if you say anything, you don't say anything."

Stunned, Jorie asked, "where's the evil bastard now?"

"Oh, if there's a hell, and I hope there is, that's where his carcass is frying. He crashed his motorcycle into a concrete wall – no helmet, thank god."

Jorie and Marcel leaned back on the sofa stunned and emotionally exhausted.

Chapter Sixteen

Awkward was too small a word to describe the situation when David returned to the office.

Things were very cool between them – she could see David wanted to talk, but what was there to talk about? The worst was behind them and he had failed her. And in some way, she felt she had failed him.

Nervously she entered his office. "David, I've given in my resignation. I'll be leaving at the end of the week. I just wanted you to know so you can relax." She gave a big sigh.

"Jorie, can we go somewhere after work and talk?"

"What is there to talk about David? I don't want to be second best. I want someone who loves me first. Who isn't afraid to be seen with me. I am truly sorry about your dad, but it really showed me what kind of life I would have with you. And I deserve better. It took me a lot of soul searching to realize that." She could feel hot tears pricking her eyes.

"You're a hundred percent right. I know that but..."

"There's that 'but'." She heard the phone on her desk ring. Turning, she left his office.

Jorie decided to move back into her parent's home until she found another job. They had lots of space and it would enable her to conserve some money until she had another pay check coming in. The positive side was that it was summer and she would be able to spend more time riding Mardi-Gras. She vowed to stay away from men for awhile and look after herself. Find out what she really wanted to do with her life and see if she could bring back that happy soul she had once been.

Friday was her last day at Abbotts. The staff were bent on taking her out after work for a farewell party. Her heart wasn't in it. The few times David had tried to initiate a conversation, she had shut him down. It would be too easy for her to get sucked back in. She loved him, she was sure of that, but there had to be more to a relationship than what he was offering. Or did there? Maybe if she stayed with him he would come around to being 'a normal person' – no longer at the mercy of guilt and anger. But no. Thinking this way was dangerous territory – it weakened her resolve.

The light on her phone flashed as she was packing her personal belongings into a box. The voice on the other end wasn't familiar. He introduced himself as Adam, David's brother.

Jorie's heart jolted. Her antenna went up. She hoped she wasn't in for another attack.

"Hello Jorie…I apologize for intruding on you, but I wonder if we could meet somewhere to talk. It would have to be Sunday because it's almost Shabbos and tomorrow being Saturday…"

"No need to explain. I understand. Yes, where would you like to meet?"

"There's a park not far from your office. Do you know the one? David said you sometimes went there together to eat your lunch."

David told his brother about me?

"Yes, I know the one. How about one o'clock?"

"Perfect. Thank you Jorie. I'll see you then."

After she hung up, she sat for a long time pondering the situation. Is this the way things go with couples who fall in love? Maybe she had seen too many romantic movies to recognize the reality. Or maybe people of different faiths and cultures weren't meant to fall in love. Relationships were difficult enough when people from the same backgrounds got together. But then, thinking about herself and Jace – they had very similar upbringings. His parents had loved her, but that didn't make any difference in their relationship and the way it worked out.

A faint smile crossed her face as she threw away the wilted flowers and wrapped the empty vase in some typing paper before placing it in the box. Every Monday she bought herself two pink carnations, a sprig of baby's breath and two green leaves to keep on her desk. David had once told her that he had been jealous thinking it was Jace or some other guy that gave them to her.

***

Sunday morning, she woke up with a stomach ache – it was nerves. *I hope like hell he isn't going to show up with his sister Ruth! I'll just walk away if he does. What can he want to talk about? Did David not tell him that we're finished? That I won't trouble them again? Oh crap! I should have taken Hella up on her offer to come with me.*

Jorie arrived at the park a few minutes early to compose herself. She was careful to dress modestly out of respect. But it was a warm day and combined with her nerves, she could feel a rivulet of perspiration running between her breasts. Breathe in, breathe out, she repeated over and over like a mantra. She picked a dandelion and found a bench under a tree in the shade and spread her skirt neatly around her. The milky dandelion sap was making her fingers stick together so she crushed in nervously and threw it away.

She recognized him by his garb as he hastened along the path towards her. The black jacket over the white shirt, black pants and black shoes. White tzitzis strings hanging down. Instead of a black hat, he had a kippah on his head. The first thing Jorie noticed was how dissimilar he looked from David. Not unpleasant, around the same height as David, but where David had a chiseled swarthy face and was tall and muscular, Adam's face was narrow, pale with a mustache, his payos framing a reddish bushy beard and stern looking wire rimmed glasses. She jumped up from the bench and went to extend her hand when she remembered Hella's words, 'religious males are forbidden from touching women other than their wives'.

"Jorie, I hope I didn't keep you waiting too long." His voice was soft and pleasant and belied the severity of his look. She breathed a sigh of relief.

"Not at all. It's a beautiful day and I was just enjoying the stillness."

He nodded and gave a slight smile. He's probably nervous too, Jorie thought.

"May I?" he asked indicating the bench. The bench was maybe five feet long and he perched so close to the end of the seat, Jorie was afraid he would fall off. She herself moved closer to her end.

Clearing his throat he began, "Well, I guess you'd like to know why I asked for this meeting. It's highly unusual, as I'm sure you know. We rarely socialize outside our community, but I felt that this is an extreme case. I hope you understand."

Jorie swallowed, *what is he getting at?* "You want me to stay away from David, is that it? Didn't he tell you we had split up? You didn't have to come here for that."

"No, you mis-understand. I'm sorry about my sister Ruth's behavior. She took my father's death very hard and it being a murder on top of it...well, the whole family was overwhelmed to say the least. No, what I came to say, or to ask you..." he was stammering, his thoughts tumbling one over another. This was the most bizarre thing he had ever had to do and he would hate to think what the community would say about his proposal. He picked up the strings of his tzitzis and ran them through his fingers, winding them and letting them fall.

"Adam, this is an awkward situation. Please just say what you came to say."

He still hadn't met her eyes. She could see he was uncomfortable even sitting at the far end of the bench. Looking down at the ground, he scuffed his shoes against the concrete.

"I'll tell you something that isn't easy for me to say." He nervously pushed his glasses up the bridge of his nose. She noted a faint sheen of moisture on his face.

"David had a difficult childhood with my father, in the way that he is now afraid to let himself be vulnerable. He had a breakdown at the Shiva house. This breakdown has been a long time coming. I love my brother deeply – maybe he told you – he said you were a good listener – we went through a lot of hardships together and I want to see him happy, but this is something he has to go through. I would just like it if you could help see him through it."

She pulled in her chin puzzled. "Me? See him through in what way? What does he have to go through? You know, Adam, I have to say, you may see me as the villain but I'm not trying to steal David away from his religion…"

"I know that, but you also should know that if the woman isn't Jewish, the children are not considered Jewish and with a non-Jewish girlfriend, he couldn't be part of the community."

Jorie hadn't thought that far ahead. "At this point, Adam, David and I don't even have a relationship – so that seems to me a moot point. And if I can say one more thing since we're being upfront with each other, that's part of my gripe with religions. The Catholic church also wants the 'pray-ers' and their income on it's side – so if you marry a Catholic you're expected to convert to Catholicism. And to say the children won't be Jewish, isn't that akin to those who pin the unfair title of 'illegitimate or bastard' on children, who through no fault of their own are born out of wedlock? It annoys me that religions seek to punish those who choose not to conform to company policy." She paused. She was embarrassed to have unleashed her anger on him. "And now it's my turn to apologize for going on a rant."

Adam sat quietly listening, nodding his head. "David said you had strong opinions on religion… but Judaism is more than a religion, it's a way of life…"

Jorie's ire rose up again. "I understand that, but so is it for the Amish, Mormons, Islam and other religions of the world – they all use ostracization to punish members who don't conform to the moral standards of their dictates. What about the religion of humanity? Of forgiveness, kindness and acceptance?"

Adam could see they had reached an impasse. "Jorie, with all due respect, I didn't come here to argue the semantics of religions with you. I came to ask if you would help my brother, David, through his crisis and we can deal with any religious issues afterwards."

Jorie looked down at her hands in her lap. "But why not have a Rabbi talk with him. I'm not a psychologist, Adam. What is it you would like me to do?"

"We had a Rabbi but David was highly resistant...there is one more thing you should know. My mother... David's mother..."

Adam shifted in his seat uncomfortably – he hadn't expected to spend as much time as this was taking. He was acutely aware of the fall-out that would ensue if he was spotted sitting on the bench with this attractive girl. He was beginning to think his wife, Rachel, had been right. He was opening a wound that would have serious repercussions. Sometimes things are better left uncovered.

"Yes, what about her?" Jorie's first thought was that maybe she's got a terminal illness. But the way he said it...did David have a different birth mother?

"My mistake...it's nothing that should involve you."
"Well, you're leaving me with the feeling it's something that could involve David a great deal."

"No, no, my mistake. It's nothing. And since you've been so direct with me, I'll put it directly to you this way. Would you be willing to study a bit about Judaism so if you were invited to our house for Shabbat dinner you would be able to partake without feeling uncomfortable?"

Adam thought back to the argument he had with Rachel just before he left the house, "Ruth will never accept her."

"'Never' is a long time Rachel."

"And what about your mother? What will our friends think? You're opening a can of worms."

"He's my brother Rachel. We grew up together. I'm afraid for him. Help is wherever we can find it. I think he should know the truth because secrets have a way of exposing themselves at the worst possible times."

To go to this girl, this Jorie, was against everything he had been taught, but was not the love he had for his brother more important? Perhaps with her, David could find his path to happiness and maybe some personal peace. Maybe it was meant to be David's life's journey and whether it worked out or not, well, not every relationship is perfect, even with my own countrymen, my lantzmen. The Pa was the dividing line. While he was alive, Adam knew David would never have peace, but now was his chance and he knew he wouldn't forgive himself if he didn't help David find some happiness.

"Adam, I have a question before you leave. Why was your father so tough on David and not on you and Ruth. David told me Ruth was the apple of his eye and you were always the 'perfect' son. Why was David always picked on?"

Adam smoothed his beard with his fingers; he pulled on the knots of his tzitzis and looked around uncomfortably. She could see he was torn about revealing something deeper. "Jorie, I really have to go. Perhaps another time. Thank you. Nice to meet you. I hope you'll give some consideration to what I said." He was becoming a nervous wreck and needed time to think about where all this was going to lead before he brought the roof down on all their heads.

***

Jorie's heart beat a tattoo in her chest. How many times had she picked up the receiver and put it down again. Did she want to start up a complicated relationship with David all over again? She loved him, but was she ready to face an uphill battle. *Shouldn't a relationship be easier? Fun even?* And something Adam had said kept reverberating in her mind. 'My mother and David's mother'. What was that about?

She steeled herself with a strong cup of coffee and picked up the phone.

It rang several times and she was just about to hang up in both relief and disappointment when he picked up. At the sound of his voice, her resolve melted.

Swallowing hard, she said, "Hi David, it's me. Would you like to get together so we can talk?"

There was a long pause on his end and Jorie was sure it had been a mistake to call. When he heard her voice on the other end of the phone, it took him a moment to find the words.

"I'd like that. Do you want to come to my apartment?"

"Be there in ten."

The spring air still had a bite in it so she grabbed a jacket and walked resignedly out the door, locking it behind her.

Driving there she had time to think. *What am I doing opening up the wounds again? How can Adam possibly think I can help David? It's one thing to be supportive, but then again, I was supportive! – it was him that fought against me. Crap!*

The person who opened the door wasn't David; she was shocked at his appearance. A shaggy mess of hair, a dark five o'clock shadow on his chin and deep circles under his eyes spoke volumes. Baggy jogging pants hung off his hips and a ripped tee-shirt covered his torso. So totally out of sync with his usual fastidiousness.

"You look like a wreck!" she exclaimed.

"You don't," he said softly. "Please, come in."

The silence was uncomfortable as he led her into the living room.

Taking in the sparse furniture, clothes strewn about on boxes of books, a few dishes on the floor next to the sofa, she commented. "Nice job you've done keeping up the place."

His eyes looked so sad, she could have kicked herself.

Trying for a recovery, "what's happening at the office? My replacement? Is she as good as I was?" Jorie asked absently while glancing around the room, anywhere but at David. The feelings of wanting to hold him and comfort him were beginning to break down her defenses.

"She's much more efficient and *really* good looking."

"...What?" Shocked, she looked at David and caught the sad mischievous grin on his face. It made her laugh and suddenly the awkwardness between them disappeared.

"Adam told me he spoke to you. It was hard for me to believe. It must have taken a great deal of guts for him to go against..."

"He's very nice David – straight forward, and he loves you deeply. He really wants you to get better. He understands what you're going through. He even said,

164

'David's not a weak person. He's been strong all his life, but even the strongest trees snap sometime.'"

David's eyes welled up. He turned his head away.

At that moment, Jorie realized how difficult it was for him to accept kindness and praise from someone. It tugged at her heart strings to see his misery.

"Come," she said, taking hold of his wrist and leading him into his bedroom. Going to the closet, she took a shirt out and handed it to him. 'C'mon, let's get you back on your feet Mr. G.Q. – personally I don't mind the scruffy woodsman look, but change that rag of a tee shirt and let's go outside and get some sun and fresh air."

As David moved to his bedroom dresser, Jorie began picking up dishes and taking them to the kitchen sink speaking loudly. "I take it you didn't go to the office today? Mr. Abbott is a nice man, but he's not going to be patient forever."

"I spoke to him and told him I needed a few weeks leave of absence. He was very understanding but said he could only give me two more weeks." They walked to the front door.

"Okay, so two weeks is better than nothing. What are you going to do with your time?"

"I was hoping we could spend some of it together."

"I didn't have a chance to tell you, but I found another job. I begin next week. It's with a new ad agency. I'm starting as a junior sales rep until I learn the ropes."

"Hey, that's great! I'm really happy for you." He managed to muster a wide grin. "You planning to give Abbott some competition?

"It's just a start-up. I doubt Abbott has to worry. So now that we have that out of the way, what are we going to do about you? Let's go to the park where we can sit on a bench and watch the ducks with their chicks."

"Ducklings you mean."

"I said ducklings."

"No you didn't, you said chicks."

"I did? Oh, well, I meant ducklings."

He gave her a sideways smile.

In the car, neither of them spoke, but David reached for her hand and held it as if he was grasping a life preserver.

They pulled into the parking lot and walked in silence until they arrived at the man-made lake. Settling themselves on a bench, David took Jorie's hand and this time felt her resist.

"I don't think that's a good idea right now," although the feel of his broad hand on hers was just what she wanted. David acted like he was stung. His defensive wall shot up.

"David, Can you understand, I'm not rejecting you, it's just..."

"You don't have to explain." His voice had turned cold as ice.

She was beginning to realize what a huge mistake it had been moving in together that first time – how different they were as people, how badly damaged his psyche had been. At the most miniscule hint of rejection or criticism, all his repressed rage flared. Why hadn't she seen that before? She had let the romantic notion of love, and lust, if she were honest, blind her from the reality. He told her she wouldn't understand his world and now it smacked her in the face once again. He had been telling the very truth.

She glanced sideways at his profile. His jaw was clenched tight and lines of anger appeared between his eyes. *Am I supposed to say something...like what?* It was as if an impenetrable wall went up between them.

She sat there looking at the bucolic scene in front of them. Weeping willow branches skimming the surface of the soft rippling water. Ducks and geese glided by with their fluff-ball babies paddling furiously in their wake. It was as relaxing a scene as one could hope for and yet the tension emanating from his body was palpable – *and all because I didn't want to hold his hand?*

"Alright, well I suppose we better be getting back," Jorie said with a sigh. "I'll just come in to get my purse," she said, wishing she would have taken it with her to the park so she could avoid an awkward parting. As she walked towards the door, he touched her arm.

"I'm sorry about what happened back there. I don't know what comes over me," he said, massaging his forehead with his fingers.

"David, your whole face changes – it's as if a blackness takes over – even your eyes get black. What goes through your mind?"

"I don't know."

"Well, you better try and figure it out. You wear your silence and anger like a shield and I'm not sure if I have what you need to help you penetrate it."

"Can you stay for some coffee?"

"Honestly, no. I find your moodiness exhausting frankly."

"I'm truly sorry. It won't happen again. I promise!"

"David, nothing has changed since we were first together. I understand you are sorry, but I think you need some professional help. And nothing will change if you don't allow yourself to be vulnerable and face the deep wound festering inside you."

"Fine. Go ahead and leave then." And the cloak of blackness descended like an iron curtain once again.

"Understand…I'm not going to be the receptacle for your anger. Think about where this rage is coming from and when you're ready to talk, you know where to reach me."

Driving home Jorie was fraught with complicated feelings. The old saying, love isn't supposed to hurt kept reverberating in her mind. Love…what an absurdly simple four letter, complicated word.

***

She had avoided telling David exactly where she was starting her new job. She knew it would set him off but she couldn't keep it a secret forever. Right now she just wanted to help him get back on his feet. After seeing him, she realized he was in a deep depression, but what could she do? Especially when he constantly shut down every time he felt her probe into whatever his problem was. She decided to make an effort to do as Adam suggested. She would learn a bit about the perimeters of Judaism, although it went against everything she believed, but, she told herself, it's always interesting to learn about other religions – look at it as a study project.

***

The phone rang in her bedroom. It had been a week since she last saw David. Why did her heart always jump at the sound of his voice.

"How's the new job going?" he asked as if nothing had happened when they last parted.

"It'll take some time to see where I fit in, but so far it's okay. And you? What have you been up to?"

"I've been thinking, walking mostly. Marcel came over a few times. We talked. I forgot what a good friend he is."

That's really good news, Jorie thought. Marcel was pragmatic and understood David's background having grown-up the same way. He would be able to empathize with David in a way Jorie could never do.

"Anyway, Adam extended an invitation and wondered if maybe you would like to come to Shabbat dinner this Friday with me?" He paused, unsure of what her reaction would be. "You don't have to if you don't want to. No pressure."

"I think I would like that. But… Ruth isn't going to be there, is she?"

"No, she and Irv are thinking about moving to Toronto – he has family there and his practice is already established, so they're busy going back and forth."

"Okay then." Jorie breathed a sigh of relief. *Good news on that front!*

"We have to be there around 7:00 – if you feel comfortable, I'll go to schul with Adam and you can get to know Rachel, his wife. Leave your car at my place and we'll walk over – you're not supposed to drive on Shabbos," he quickly clarified.

Oh god, Jorie thought. What kind of reception is Rachel going to give me?

"I'll go, but David, I don't want to be attacked."

"Don't worry, Adam assured me.

Chapter Seventeen

She was excited about starting her new job. Jace had promised her her own office and no hanky panky between them. But there was a lot to be done before they actually opened for business. Jorie was kept busy assigning and arranging furniture to the different office spaces. Filing cabinets and a filing system had to be set up. Jace already had lined up new clients and he wanted things in order quickly so they could get down to business and make back the money he was investing.

She and David had been in phone contact daily, but by the end of the day, she was so tired she just wanted to drop into bed.

"Be patient, just another week and I should have more time," she assured him.

She was sitting on the floor sorting through files, when Jace came over with another man wanting to introduce her. Plunking the files on the floor beside her, she stood up and offered her hand.

"Jorie, this is Chris Daniels. He's a partner in the company and our sales rep. general manager. You're going to be working alongside him learning the ropes. I've already given him your creds... beautiful, brilliant and eager."

Jorie blushed – she felt confused. She was flattered but at the same time flustered that he painted a rather shallow portrait of her to the person she had to work with. "Brilliant is definitely hyperbole, but what about my experience and charming personality?"

"Yeah, yeah...and that too," Jace said dismissively. "I'll leave you two to get better acquainted."

Chris gave Jorie a sympathetic smile as Jace walked off. "I can see you're in the middle of something right now. How about we grab a bite to eat after we're finished for the day and you can tell me about your experience working at Abbott and a little bit about your goals."

At dinner that evening, they ended up talking for hours. Chris was well travelled, twenty-eight years old and single. And kind.

"How come you're not married?" Jorie asked.

"I guess I just haven't met the right girl yet."

Jorie assessed him from across the table. He was a few inches taller than her height of five foot six. He had beautiful dark lashed hazel eyes, a pleasant face and thick sandy brown hair. And he was calm and soft-spoken. She needed calmness. Her mind was always going a mile a minute. It was her biggest weakness. Unless the subject was something that really interested her, her mind tended to wander to all sorts of ideas and trivial thoughts like where the edge of infinity is...

At the close of the evening, she felt confident that Chris would be a good mentor and they would work well together.

***

Friday after work, she picked up a cinnamon babka from the Kosher bakery and tried to settle her nerves before driving to David's. Over and over she asked herself why she was continuing down this rock strewn path. Somewhere inside her was this innate pull and deep undefinable connection she had with David. Even if she chose not to continue the relationship, it would be as if a piece of the puzzle would forever be missing. She had a compulsion to continue and see where it lead, for better or worse.

He was waiting in the parking lot for her and his face lit up when she drove in. What a brilliant smile he has, she thought to herself smiling back at him as she backed the car into a space.

He looked so much better than the week before. He had a kippah on his head and for some reason, it touched her and she thought it made him look even more handsome with his dark hair and eyes. She let him embrace her and they held each other for a long time. She wished it could be this simple. If they never had to talk, she could stay in his arms and be contented.

Walking towards Adam's house, she told him about her new job and he filled her in on Abbott news. Hella and Vicky kept her pretty much informed, but she was pleased to see David chatting so freely. His spirits seemed to have lifted considerably.

They entered through the back door into the kitchen. Adam was drying dishes at the sink but came over and greeted them warmly – without touching. Smells of delicious food unfamiliar to Jorie permeated the air.

Rachel came out of the pantry carrying a casserole dish. Jorie was surprised – she hadn't known what to expect - after her experience with Ruth, she had conjured up a witchy looking woman with a sour mouth ready to pounce on her. Rachel was none of that. Heavily pregnant, a robust attractive looking woman of about Jorie's age, a pretty blondish wig framing her heart shaped face, natural pink cheeks and blue eyes gave her a soft appearance.

Placing the casserole on the counter, she greeted David and then Jorie with a reserved half smile. Inwardly Jorie cringed.

David said to Jorie, "Adam and I are going to shul. We won't be long," he touched her arm briefly – a fleeting reassurance, as he and Adam exited.

Sure, run off and leave me. What am I going to talk to her about? Why did I even come. I feel like I'm trapped in a bad play.

"Can I help with anything? Congratulations — ah… Mazeltov on the baby."

"Thank you. No, everything is fine. So tell me Jorie, how did you and David meet?" Rachel asked, her back to Jorie as she worked at the counter.

So, cut right to the chase. "We worked together at the same ad agency and just became friends."

"I see."

Jorie could feel the tension emanating between them — or maybe it was just her. She had anticipated something bad and now she was imagining it. Her stomach was churning. Anyway, she told herself, if she goes after me, I can walk out and back to my car. She couldn't figure out how to start a conversation in a more pleasant way.

"How do you feel about David?"

"You mean as a friend? Or…?"

"Do you see a relationship between you and David working out in the long term?"

"Ahhh, well right now, we're just, ahhh…" *Good grief, how am I supposed to answer that when I don't even know myself.*

Ruth turned around, but still stayed at the counter keeping distance between them.

"Whatever you're cooking smells really delicious."

"Thank you," Rachel said. *There's that half smile again. It never reaches her eyes.* "I just wonder if you know what you're getting yourself into with David. Adam has a big heart, but his sister and the rest of the family will never accept you."

"Well that's pretty blunt. So, would you like me to leave right now and you can explain to them why I'm not here when they come back?"

That caught her by surprise. "No, I apologize," she replied quickly. "It's really not my place to say. I just thought it would be best for you to know these things upfront." Jorie noticed the high color that had risen in Rachel's face before she turned her back and faced the counter once again.

It was now or never. *I'm invited as a guest. I don't have to put up with this. She's being a bully.* "Listen Rachel. I didn't set out to catch myself a Jewish boy. His covenant is with you and his family and it's his choice if he wants to step outside it. I'm not forcing him to like me. And really, I'm already aware of how closed your religion is and other than coming to experience a pleasant Shabbat dinner, I have no other motive. And anything else, is between David and myself. If you want more information about his or my personal life, please, feel free to ask him."

Jorie's heart was thudding. She wasn't a confrontational person but the tension had pushed her over the edge. Actually she was amazed and kind of pleased with herself that she had the courage to stand up. After that, Rachel's attitude changed for the better. "Yes, you're absolutely right. I'm going to light the Shabbos candles now. You're welcome to join me if you like."

Shortly after, David and Adam came in the door along with another young couple and their two small children.

Adam made the introductions. "Aryeh," who nodded discreetly in her direction, "and Charna Amsler, this is Jorie Fielding, David's friend." The two small children peeked out from behind their parents. Aryeh's eyes avoided hers, but Charna gave her a warm smile and Jorie thought maybe it was a good thing that these people were also there so she didn't have to feel like a bug under a microscope.

As the dinner proceeded, Charna helped Rachel, working as one, obviously completely comfortable with each other, clearing the table and bringing out the next courses and Jorie felt free to sit and observe. She had been moved by the ritual songs and different blessings and prayers…and seeing a side of David comfortable in his own milieu.

Thanking Rachel as she and David were leaving, Charna came over, put a hand on her arm and said, "it was nice to meet you Jorie. I'm glad you were able to join us." After all the tension, Jorie felt like hugging her in gratitude. It was awful to feel so thankful to someone just because they were nice to you.

Walking back to David's, he asked her what she thought of the whole evening.

"You want the brutal truth or the sanitized version?"

"Give it to me with both barrels."

"Well, Rachel and I had a 'go-round' before you came back from shul. I don't think we'll ever be friends. I also told you that I think ritual is nice to read about – and I enjoyed observing it, but David, I could never practice or live like that. It's just too repressive for me. I mean, everything is so regimented, so strictly laid-out. If you're raised like that, how can you possibly ever think for yourself? And you were brought up like this?"

"It wasn't all that bad, was it?"

"Yes, for me it was. Apart from Charna and Adam, had I not felt the weight of judgement directed at me I would have enjoyed it. I'm not sure what this is supposed to accomplish, but I wouldn't want to go through it again."

"Look, it was the first time Rachel met you. Let her get to know you a little better and she'll see what I see in you."

"I really don't think so. I'm an outsider to their world, an intruder and unless I decided to convert and adhere to their rules and regimens I'll never fit in. Even if I wanted to, I can't be like them – it's just not in my nature."

"So, where does that leave us?"

"You tell me, David. You have to decide what's most important to you. I'm not going to live a double life and I'm not interested in taking on, what I see, as a repressive …." She stopped before she said something she would regret.

"Okay, I can see you're upset. I appreciate you trying."

They parted tensely. She knew David felt sad that things hadn't gone better. But once she was in her car a weighted mantel dropped off her shoulders and driving home she could only feel she had been freed. He wanted to see her on the weekend, but she begged off saying she had errands to run now that she was working again and Sunday she promised to go with her mother to visit her grandmother. The fact was, she needed time to herself to think about the relationship and where it was going. Because at this point, it was going nowhere.

***

Monday morning was fast in coming. The office was finally looking organized and Chris greeted her with fresh coffee and a sweet roll.

"Bless you Chris. You really know the way to a girl's heart."

Chris smiled. "I thought we could go through some of the files today and lay out a plan as to who we're going to tackle with some cold calls." They both grabbed an armful of folders and made their way to the boardroom where they could spread everything out.

She liked working with Chris. He was patient and never made her feel as if her questions were stupid. They had their heads together making notes when Jace walked in. Right away, Jorie glanced up and saw the look on his face. Jealousy was written all over it. His jaw clenched. She knew that clench. It happened when he was getting tense or angry.

"Well, you two look pretty chummy together. Accomplishing anything or just getting to know each other better?"

"What does that mean?" Jorie spoke too fast, an edge to her voice. He had promised her there would be business only between them and she didn't need to hear any jabs.

Jace ignored her question focusing his eyes on Chris. "When you're finished here, can I see you in my office, Chris. Thanks." He turned on his heel and left.

They worked until three o'clock, ordering in sandwiches and coffee. Several times Jace had walked by pretending not to look through the glass window, but Jorie caught his sideways glance. Finally, he stuck his head in the door. "Did you forget I asked to see you in my office Chris?"

"What?" Chris gave him a perplexed look. "Is it something urgent? You said when we're finished here. We're not finished."

Half an hour later, after they cleaned up the boardroom, Chris went down the hall to Jace's office.

"What's going on?"

Jace got up from his desk and approached Chris. "I think I made it clear when we decided to hire Jorie that she was off limits."

"So?"

"You two looked mighty cozy in there."

Chris couldn't believe his ears. "Jace, she and I are supposed to work together. It's our first week. Are you telling me you're going to act like a jealous fool every time we're out of the office on a call together? C'mon man."

"I just don't want you hitting on her, that's all." Jace turned and walked back to his desk plunking into his chair like a sulky child.

"You better get over yourself, man. You don't own her and this partnership is not going to work if you keep up the attitude. There's a lot of work we need to get done if we're going to be successful and I don't need you acting like a spoiled baby. You want to let her go and bring on somebody else, fine with me, but she has potential…and another thing, I'm not some lackey you summon – we're equal financial partners and don't you forget it. "

"Yeah, yeah, okay. I hear ya," Jace interrupted. Chris turned abruptly and stormed out of his office.

Later that day Chris pulled Jorie aside. "Are you sure you and Jace are through?"

"I'm one hundred percent sure."

"Well maybe you should tell him that. I think he still has a thing for you and it's going to make us working together a trifle difficult."

Jorie was steamed. She liked Chris and they were working well together. Marching into Jace's office, she confronted him. "You promised there would be no 'you and me' if I took this job. I took you at your word and now you're harassing Chris? I've moved on Jace and I've heard through the grapevine you have a new girlfriend. Why can't that be enough for you?"

Jace looked down at the blotter on his desk. The muscle in his cheek was working. "maybe it was a mistake bringing you on here," he said quietly

"What?!" Jorie couldn't believe her ears. "You're going to punish me because of your own stupid insecurities? Screw you Jace Patterson. You can go to hell as far as I'm concerned." She turned and flew out of his office before the welling tears could overflow.

Going to her desk, she began gathering her things shoving them into her bag. Chris came over. "What happened in there? I heard you yelling."

"He's such an asshole. I should have known he wouldn't let go. All about his macho ego. What a loser." Her hands were shaking.

"Can we go somewhere for coffee so you can calm down. I hate to lose you so quickly. Why don't you go home for a couple days. I'll speak to Jace and we'll work things out."

"I can't Chris. Thanks anyway. I'll be fine – I just need to be alone. I enjoyed our brief time together."

Leaving the building, her mind was a whirlwind and her heart kept elevating, unnerving her even more. She felt like running or pounding on something. Instead she went home, changed and drove out to the farm to ride Mardi-Gras.

Immediately, as she stepped out of the car, the smell of horses and hay brought her senses under control. Brushing the horse and saddling him up was calming. Riding him through the pasture, the squeak of the saddle leather, Mardi's ears twitching at all the sights and sounds, the power of his muscles moving forward under her, the feel of his sleek neck – it was brilliant. Nothing brought her more peace than riding this beautiful animal.

She leaned forward and hugged his neck. Mardi was one male that never let her down.

***

"I lost my job," she told David the next evening as she entered his apartment.

"So fast? You were only there four days?"

He had called and asked if they could get together and he promised to be on his best behavior.

"I guess I didn't tell you," she said, removing her jacket and throwing it on a chair. " It was Jace that hired me – he started his own ad agency. Nothing going on between us," she injected quickly as she walked into the kitchen to get a glass of water. "He had his partner, Chris, training me to be a sales rep and would you believe, that idiot, Jace, got jealous!" She was getting all riled up again.

She didn't notice the look that crossed David's face.

"You went to work for your ex, Jace? When were you planning to tell me this interesting little piece of news?"

"I didn't want to have a fight over it. I needed a job. The salary was almost double what I was making and I had a real chance to get ahead. It was a no-brainer. Except for that asshole had to go and ruin it." Taking the water, she returned to the living room and sat down on the sofa. David was walking in slow circles.

"Let's go over this again. You went to work with your ex-boyfriend and didn't think it was important enough to tell me?"

"David, can you get off it, please! I've had enough of stupid men and their frail little egos – there's nothing, no feelings, nada on my part for that man. Strictly business, until he chose to make it something else. Tsk." She gave a big sigh. "And now, he leaves me a message that he wants me to come back. What does he think I am?"

David stopped walking. "You're not going back are you?"

"I haven't decided yet. The money is better than I would get somewhere else…and I liked what I was starting to learn…I don't know."

"I don't want you going back," he bristled.

"Huh? …Haven't you been listening to me? I said I have no feelings for him."

She noticed he was tensing up. That usually was the prelude to an explosion.

"You know, I thought I could tell you and you might give me some support and insight so I could work things through. But instead you're getting all testy over NOTHING! – I should have talked to Hella. Why would I expect a man to understand anything that isn't to his own benefit. Good grief!"

She picked up her jacket and strode towards the door.

"Jorie, wait," he said, grasping her wrist and pulling her back. "It's just that… okay well, if I have to admit it, I'm jealous. I'm jealous that you were in a relationship with him and that I'm not…I'm not…"

"Not what David?"

"Not good enough for you!" he blurted out.

"Oh my god, you stupid man! What are you talking about?" She looked up at his troubled face and shook her head. "You're so much more than Jace could ever hope to be. What I feel for you, I never felt for Jace. Don't you know that?" Seeing his vulnerability softened her resolve. Putting her arms around him, she leaned her head against his chest. "But you're a lot of trouble, you know," she muttered into his shirt.

"I know I am, but come, sit a minute," he said, leading her to the sofa. "I have something to ask you."

Jorie briefly shut her eyes. *What is he going to hit me with now?*

"Rachel had her baby, a boy, and they're having the Bris tomorrow. I was wondering if you would come with me?"

"Ooo, I know what that is. That's where they cut the piece off the little pischer's petsel."

David laughed at her Yiddish. 'It's called circumcision. But yes, basically that's it. From whence are you picking up the Yiddish words?"

"Not from whence, from Hella," she giggled. "We use them a lot. I like Yiddish. It's very descriptive in a whimsical way."

That was one of the things David loved, and feared about Jorie. He never knew what was going to pop out of her mouth.

"I have to go David. My mother said she was pleased to have me move back, but I have to do my own laundry - a month's worth and I have to get to it."

"Oy!" He exclaimed, mock slapping both sides of his face. "So you're no 'baleboosteh' I take it," he raised his eyebrows mischievously.

"That one I haven't heard. What means that — Bal-a-busta?"

"Mistress of the house…a good housekeeper."

"For sure I am no bal-a-busta."

She left muttering the word, marking it to memory to surprise Hella with.

***

Arriving home, she checked the answering machine and saw Jace had left several messages asking her to come back to the office to talk. This was getting tedious and emotionally exhausting. She thought about all the while they were going together how she had catered to his ego afraid he might get tired of her or cheat with someone, which he did, so it didn't really matter whichever way she played it. It was only about the chase and assuaging his ego. The way to keep him was to never let him have her. *How bizarre and tiresome.* That was his character – it really had nothing to do with her. Why did she have to see things so clearly always after the fact?

But, and there's always a but – it's a real opportunity to learn the advertising business from the bottom up. She liked working with Chris and the money was good. *So what if Jace makes some snide comments. Just brush them off. Eventually he'll get the hint – especially if we get busy. Besides, I'm not working with him. And if he really causes me problems, I can leave with some experience under my belt and look elsewhere for another job.*

Putting the laundry in the drier, she picked up the phone and dialed his home number.

Chapter Eighteen

What to wear, what to wear she mumbled to herself scrolling through her closet the next morning. *Black skirt, pink blouse and black jacket. I should be safe with that. Oh yes, and a bobby pin and doily for my head. Wouldn't want to offend anyone.* She was nervous. *His family are so rigid and there are so many rules. How do they get so many people to follow them all? My mind would feel constipated – on the other hand, you don't have to think or make any real decisions. Everything is laid out for you from morning till night. And if you're with a bunch of like-minded people, you're all in sync. I could maybe see where it has it's appeal.*

Checking her make-up and hair in the mirror one last time, she got in the car and drove over to David's. He was outside in the parking lot leaning against a concrete divider.

Pulling into a spot, she turned the car off and stepped out exclaiming, "Wow! David you look so handsome, all spiffed up."

"You're not so shabby yourself," he replied, giving her a warm embrace. Taking her hand he walked her towards his car.

This was the David she had first fallen for. "Seriously, I'm so glad you're feeling better."

"I've done a lot of self-reflecting and I have to give my brother, Adam, credit for his open mindedness. To be liberal in his thinking goes against everything he was raised with, but he's very pragmatic about some things and I know he wants the best for me. We've had some interesting talks. I have to bite the bullet and deal with the consequences – for better or worse."

"I like this new David, but what brought this on?" she said, giving his hand a squeeze.

"Part of my problem growing up was I never had the desire that Adam and Ruth had for practicing and studying religion. Even then, I remember thinking I wanted to be free to do other things – things that went against the perimeters of what I was being taught. But at the same time, there was the guilt of not being able to live up to my father's expectations. I felt like an outsider who didn't fit in. Like you did at the Shabbat dinner."

"So, how does this revelation affect us?"

"I have to work on myself. My father is gone. His judgement was what I could never get by. My mother will always love me and she doesn't have to answer to him anymore. It will take time. I hope you'll give me a chance to prove myself."

Jorie wanted more than anything to give him a chance, but only time would tell if his words had any weight to them.

∗∗∗

The room in the basement of the synagogue was already packed with people when they arrived. David led her through the crowd to where Adam was standing.

"Mazeltov big brother," David said, shaking Adam's hand vigorously and hugging him with his other arm. Jorie stifled a giggle at the fact that David was so much more buff, not to mention a few inches taller than Adam and yet affectionally called him 'big brother'.

"Mazeltov Adam," Jorie said shyly. She felt incredibly out of place with all the black hats and women staring at her. Or maybe they were just curious about a new face in the crowd. *I shouldn't be so quick to judge.*

"Where's the good little mother?" David inquired.

"You know how it is, she can't bear to hear him cry, so she's in the back over there with Ruth and Ma."

Jorie's antenna went up when she heard Ruth's name mentioned. Unconsciously she glanced to the back of the room and her eyes locked with Ruth's. She had vowed to herself that no matter how nervous she felt, she wasn't going to babble and she wasn't going to allow herself to be intimidated. Keep quiet and stay composed she told herself.

Men were coming to shake David's hand and nodded at her, curiosity in their eyes. She gave a faint smile in return but she was beginning to have that feeling again of being a dissected insect. To her dismay, she saw Ruth walking towards them. Quickly she asked David where the Ladies Room was and made herself scarce in the other direction.

Her heart thudded as she pushed the door open. *How long can I stay in here?* It was pretty luxurious for a bathroom, she thought, taking it in. There was a comfy patterned sofa and two chairs near a mirrored wall and lovely marble sinks with gold-tone faucets. Some of the women coming in and going out gave her puzzled looks, others smiled and nodded in a friendly way. One kind woman stopped and asked her if she was alright – if she needed anything. *Does everybody know everyone here? Do I look so out of place? Or is it just my imagination? Why do I feel so intimidated? Well, I can't stay in here forever.*

Tentatively she made her way back to David. The ceremony was over and people were filing into another room for the celebratory Kiddush.

"Everything okay?" he inquired seeing her pale face.

"Yes. It's just seeing Ruth unnerved me."

"She'll be fine, don't worry about her. Come, let's get some food in our stomachs."

They filled their plates at the buffet and took their seats at a table. A woman came across the room towards Jorie. She looked familiar but she couldn't quite place her.

"Hi Jorie…Charna Amsler. Remember we met you at Adam and Rachels?"

"Oh yes. Hi! I'm sorry I didn't recognize you, I just didn't expect to know anyone here."

"How are you? Is this your first bris?" she said with a sincere smile.

"It is. Unfortunately I missed the important part of the ceremony. I wasn't feeling too well and was in the bathroom during the big moment."

"I think a lot of people don't feel too well when they see the knife near the little guy's do-hickey — especially men."

They both laughed at that. Immediately Jorie's guard went down. Here was somebody who wasn't judging her and she could relate to. David greeted Charna and then asked if he could be excused to go and speak to someone on the other side of the room. "Do you mind if I leave you for a few minutes?" He put a reassuring hand on Jorie's shoulder.

"No, please, go ahead." If Charna hadn't come along, she definitely would have minded. "Would you like to sit down?" Jorie asked, pulling out the empty chair next to her.

"I would," she said, taking the seat. "I was sorry we didn't get more time to chat at the Shabbat dinner. I could see how uncomfortable you were and wanted to reassure you. You know, you're not the only person who has gone through this. My sister fell in love with a Christian man. She and I were very close and there was hell to pay at home. It was a very traumatic time," she swallowed, and her eyes looked beyond Jorie, remembering. "I knew the relationship was going on but didn't tell my parents. I met him a few times secretly; he was a doctor surgeon and I liked him and I could see they were very much in love — it always starts that way in the gentile world, doesn't it — I mean, falling in love rather than being matched.

Anyway, that was five years ago. They ran off and got married. My father's rath chased them right out of the country. My mother was devastated by the whole thing.

They live in California now and have two adorable children, a boy and a girl, my niece and nephew, who I'll probably never see and she won't see mine. We write occasionally and send pictures, but I feel guilty, betraying my parents wishes…it's difficult." Her chin puckered a bit and Jorie placed her hand on Charna's to keep her from crying.

"It changed a lot of my beliefs in our religion. I'm happy enough with Aryeh and I love our kids, but I often wonder what the whole thing is about when religion brings so much pain to people."

"I've thought about that a lot too. I think most religions are based on inherent good, but the self-appointed enforcers are the ones that cause the strife. I'm sorry you and your sister were forced apart Charna. I hope there will come a time when you and she can reunite and introduce the cousins to each other. It was nice of you to relate your story to me. Perhaps we need another cup of coffee?"

"Yes and let's get a second piece of that decadent cake to go with it. Cake at 11:30 in the morning – I love it," Charna laughed. That was something they had no trouble agreeing on.

David was preoccupied chatting with some men while she and Charna went to the sweet table. Jorie cut a slice off a rich looking torte and placed it on her plate. A loud whisper in her ear and a strong whiff of alcohol caused her to freeze.

"What are you doing here?" Ruth hissed. Jorie quickly turned towards the voice. Her heart almost jumped out of her throat. Ruth's face had a twisted look. With a swoop of her fingers she knocked the plate out of Jorie's hand. It clattered to the floor attracting everyone's attention. "You're trying to humiliate our family? Is that it? My brother – my half-brother I should say, killed my father and now he wants to kill my mother. The mother who loved him even though his mother was a tramp? He was lucky my father took him in. You should go with him. You should both LEAVE! You're both not one of us! That's why he was so much trouble. His mother was a piece of trash!" Ruth was screeching and dead silence hung in the room.

Jorie stood there stunned and mortified to be the center of attention. Faces staring at her. Everything moving in slow motion. Would the moment never end? She heard Charna's voice call to Adam and David as she put her arm protectively around Jorie. Suddenly they were there and Ruth's husband Irv was leading Ruth away, apologizing for the scene saying she had too much to drink.

All eyes are on me, the outsider, the invader, the pariah. Jorie was frozen to the spot. Charna took one arm and David the other and led her down the hallway to an unoccupied room where they sat down.

Charna was the first to speak. "I'm so sorry that had to happen – please believe me, we're not all like her."

David held her hand. He was beside himself with fury that Ruth had attacked her in such a public way. "Just sit here a few minutes and then we'll leave," he said trying to sort through the whole mess. He had caught only a few words that Ruth was screaming but they were beginning to reverberate in his mind. 'His mother was a tramp?' Did he really hear that? 'You're lucky my father took you in' ?

Adam pushed open the door and stepped into the room. "There you are. I've been searching all over."

Having Adam there, Charna excused herself. "Jorie...if you need me..." she said, pointing towards the hall. She quietly closed the door behind her.

"Adam, what the hell was that all about? I never want to see that bitch again. I don't care if she is my sister. She was always a snide little... even when we were kids, she always had it out for me. And what was that about *my* mother? Where is Ma anyway?"

"I told Rachel to stay with her until I come back. David, we need to clear some things up, but not now. I have to try and smooth things over out there – we don't need everyone in our business. Why don't you take Jorie to your place and I'll stop by later."

"I'd like to go home David. I just want to get out of here," Jorie said.

Arriving at David's place to pick up her car, David said, "I'd really like you to stay here with me for a little while until we both calm down. I'm still in shock like you are. We can have some coffee and try and unwind."

"You better make it decaf. I'm jittery enough."

Closing the apartment door behind him, he went to put the water on for coffee. Jorie plopped onto the sofa and sat there replaying the scene in her mind. *What had Ruth said? His mother was a tramp? Lucky their father took him in? She actually knocked the plate* **right out** *of my hand! That woman has a serious problem!*

Placing the coffee on the table, David sat down beside her. Neither one spoke for several minutes until Jorie finally broke the ice.

"Did you hear any of what Ruth said?"

"Something about my mother not being my mother...and...and, my **real** mother was a tramp? Not being one of us?"

190

"Do you know anything about that?"

"Not a thing, but I sure as hell want to find out."

"David, are you positive you want to know? It might not be something so easy to accept." Jorie remembered his fragile state of mind when his father died. "If you don't mind, I'd prefer to go home. I'll come back tomorrow morning and maybe Adam will have called by then."

After Jorie left, David was too agitated to sleep. He changed his clothes and drove to Adam's. The lights were all off in the house except for the one in Adam's study. Rather than ring the bell and wake everyone up, he knocked at the door hoping Adam would hear.

Opening the door a crack, Adam peered out and saw it was David. "C'mon in – I guess neither of us could sleep."

"I still have so much adrenalin and anger, I couldn't wait for morning."

"Come," Adam said, turning and leading the way – "you want something to drink?"

Adam looked even paler than usual, David noted, as he led the way to his office.

"No. I just want answers. That batshit crazy sister of ours wrecked your whole..."

"David," Adam held up a hand. "Irv apologized and said Ruth has been drinking a lot lately, but he never expected her to get out of control like she did. She hasn't been able to get pregnant and he thinks that's what led to her anger and outburst."

David pondered this bit of news. For a religious woman not to be able to have kids was a serious problem in their community. *But still...*

"So are you telling me what she said about *my* mother was made-up?"

Adam swallowed. Getting up he went to the bookshelves, reached underneath into the back, brought out a bottle he had been saving and poured two shot glasses of Glenfiddich 12 year old Scotch.

"Drink."

David didn't really like the taste of Scotch, but something told him he might be needing the fortification.

"Don't just swallow it. Hold it in your mouth for ten seconds and then swallow slowly."

David choked a little, but it wasn't so bad. "Since when did you become an expert on drinking Scotch?" he asked in a bemused voice.

Adam nodded his head as if in deep thought. "Sometimes you just need a little extra help."

Suddenly the door to the study opened and Rachel stuck her head in. "It's one-thirty - I heard voices…Oh, David. I'll leave you two then. Goodnight."

Adam got up and poured another drink for both of them. He was very nervous about what he was going to tell David and more than that, afraid of how David was going to react. There was no way to lessen the blow.

"David, what I'm going to tell you isn't easy. But I want you to know that I'll always be here for you. You'll always be my brother no matter what."

David braced himself. He couldn't imagine what could possibly be so bad to make Adam act this nervous. Did he really want to know? Too late now.

"Do you remember when I went to New York to study at the Yeshiva and stayed with Aunt Esther?"

David ran his fingers around the neck of his t-shirt. He remembered. He was fifteen and Adam was eighteen. David had been jealous that Adam got to go by himself to New York and he had to stay at home. The Pa had made it clear that there was no way he was going to send his 'laidi-gaier', his loafing, idler son, David, to New York anytime in the future. The memory of the insult still made him cringe with hurt and humiliation.

"Well, Aunt Esther had started to imbibe a bit with Kosher wine in the evenings. Morty told me she was depressed and often had too much to drink. So one night when I came back from school, she said it wasn't fair that she had to carry the burden of a secret this big by herself, that she could no longer do it and didn't want to protect Zev anymore. She started to talk. At first I thought she was making a story up, but then I began to recollect a series of events that had taken place and I knew what she was saying must be true."

David shifted in his seat. His hand reached for the Glenfiddich in his glass. He wished Adam would get to the point and at the same time, he didn't really want to hear what he knew was coming.

"There was a period of time when the Pa had his pawn shop and he and Ma were not getting along. I remember I heard Ma scream at him and you know, she never screamed at anyone. That time, the Pa stormed out and didn't come back for several days. Aunt Esther came for a visit. I heard Ma crying when they were in a bedroom. The Pa said later that he stayed at the shop. After that, things cooled down. One morning I woke up and there was a new baby in the house. You."

"Me?" David jumped.

"At that young age, what did I know about women being pregnant. I just accepted that you were my new baby brother. Ruth, being more aware of these things knew better than me and she didn't accept the situation at all, but there was nothing she could do about it. I thought you were the cutest baby and I have to say, I loved you from the first time I saw you." Adam's cheeks flushed. They weren't accustomed to showing their emotions so overtly. "I had prayed for a brother each time Ma got pregnant, but then she miscarried, so when you arrived, I thought it was a gift especially for me from HaShem and I vowed to be the best brother I could be."

David was overcome with emotion hearing Adam express himself this way. "And you have been Adam. I couldn't have asked for a better brother…so what…?"

"So, according to Aunt Esther, the Pa had an affair with his lady bookkeeper and…"

"An affair!" David jumped in – it was the most shocking thing he could ever imagine. "The Pa had an affair?" *My straight-laced, pious father had an affair?* Never in his wildest dreams could he ever have imagined.

He took another sip of Scotch. It burned going down but that was nothing compared to the burning anger he was beginning to feel. All this time, growing up, he had put his father on a pedestal so high that all the beatings…the horrible beatings to his psyche as well as his body, he recollected now as so many thoughts were expanding and swirling through his mind…*I always thought I deserved them because my father was so perfect he would never have hit me if I didn't deserve it.*

But now, came another very loud thought. *Who is this woman, the bookkeeper?*

Adam was watching David come to grips with the information.

"Do you want me to go on? Would you prefer to wait until Jorie could be here with you?"

"No. Please just tell me. The bookkeeper wasn't Jewish was she."

"No she wasn't."

Another bombshell. "So that means, technically that I'm not Jewish either."

Adam nodded slowly.

And now, David started to remember two other strange incidents from his childhood.

"I remember a time the Pa took us to Lafontaine park far from our house. We thought it was strange and exciting because he rarely took us anywhere except to shul. We went on the bus and he brought salami sandwiches for us to eat on a bench...and then a lady showed up. She had tears in her eyes when she saw me. She tried to hug me but I pushed her away and ran to the swings. I felt uncomfortable that a stranger would touch me... and I was more interested in going on the swings – that was her, my real mother – my birth mother?"

A jumble of thoughts were tumbling through his mind, but he could never imagine having any other mother except his Ma. She was his real mother. "And another time, I happened to be looking out the window and down on the street I saw the Pa and that same woman having an argument. But nobody ever spoke about that and I didn't think any more of it."

"Yes, I didn't equate that park situation either until Aunt Esther told me that your birth mother threatened to make trouble unless she was allowed to see you."

"But why didn't she keep me?"

"She had no money to speak of and no marriage prospects – she was an orphan with no family members."

"But people must have known, seen that she was pregnant?"

"I don't remember all the details and neither did Aunt Esther, but apparently she went to a home for pregnant girls run by the nuns."

David sat there stunned trying to make sense of all this new information. "This poor woman with no relatives was forced to give up her baby...me..." David pondered that for a while rubbing his forehead with both hands. "That's so sad."

"It was the times. Think about it. She couldn't support you and she had no prospects. The Pa had always wanted more boys. But Ma kept having miscarriages - he had you circumcised and brought you home. The lady was gone and Ma, kind-hearted Ma, fell in love with you at first sight. You were always her favorite, and still are, you know that don't you?"

"But, but...did the Pa love this woman, my mother?"

"Your birth mother, you mean. I don't know if he loved the other woman or it was just something that happened because they worked together."

David took another sip of his drink. So many questions tumbling and swirling.

"And Ruth knows all this? Is my..." He had a hard time even saying the words, "birth-mother still alive?"

"Ruth was a teenager and knew something was going on when all of a sudden a new baby arrived. It pains me to say it, but she was always jealous that you were Ma's 'special child', knowing where you came from."

They sat in silence for a long time. David was reeling from all this new information and how finally a lot of pieces of the puzzle were falling into place. After a while, Adam drained his glass and rose. "Why don't you stay in the guest room overnight and we can talk more tomorrow. Things will be easier in the morning."

David tossed and turned and finally fell into a troubled sleep. Waking at 5:30 he knew he wouldn't fall back to sleep. He stumbled down the hallway to the kitchen, feeling like he was hung over. Rachel had a pot of coffee ready. She was walking up and down jiggling the baby in her arms. He didn't need to ask if she knew.

"You slept well David?"

"Everything considered...well enough," he said pouring himself a cup. He reached for the non-dairy creamer and spooned it into the hot black liquid. The coffee jolted him back to life.

"Thanks for the coffee and the room, Rachel. I have to get back to my place and get dressed for the office. Tell Adam I'll speak to him later."

Just as he was ready to exit, Rachel said, "I hope everything works out for you. Whichever way things go, we'll always be your family." David flashed her a grateful smile.

***

It was a long day, trying to focus on the many projects he had to handle and his mind constantly snapping back like an over-stretched elastic to everything Adam had told him.

When Jorie walked into his apartment after work, she took one look and knew something big had happened. The dark circles under his eyes were telling – his usually swarthy skin had a white pallor to it. She knew better than to ask him about it. He would tell her in his own time.

"Can we sit down?" Why was she asking? Usually she just made herself at home, but David seemed altered in some way. Not functioning normally. Jorie took off her sweater and threw it over the back of the kitchen chair. Helping herself to an iced tea from the fridge, "do you want one?" He nodded. She poured him half and took the two glasses and walked over to the sofa. They both sat down. David let his head loll backwards as he reached behind and rubbed his neck.

"I'm not Jewish," he said into the air.

Jorie blinked. She screwed up her face. "What does that mean?"

"My mother, my real...my birth-mother was not Jewish. Therefore," he said with emphasis, "I - am – not - Jewish."

"Okaaay." Jorie was trying to make sense of this and wished David would move along instead of making it into an infuriating riddle.

"So how did you come to be brought up Jewish?" She was chomping at the bit to ask a thousand questions, but she knew David – it had to come out in his own time, in his own way.

"I don't know where to start. I couldn't sleep after the fiasco yesterday, so I went to Adam's and he told me the whole story or as much as he knows."

"So tell me what Adam said. It's only words David. It's not going to change anything. You're still you and after the shock wears off of whatever he told you, we'll get through this together." She reached over and grasped his hand.

After David recounted the story with the details Adam had given him, he squeezed the bridge of his nose with a sigh. Jorie sat there stunned trying to unravel the information.

"Do you know if your birth-mother is still alive?"

"No, she's passed."

"That's alright then. She probably couldn't have told you anything more. It's not the first time this sort of thing has happened." She was trying to conjure up words that would be deep and especially consoling, but her mind was a blank.

"So where do you go from here?"

"It's very weird, according to the laws of Judaism I'm not technically Jewish, but I still think I'm Jewish. Do I just erase all my past, forget all my learning, cast off my tallis and kippah and walk out? A clean slate ready to start over again? Adam is still my brother – half brother now and Ruth my half sister. Well, at least she can't throw anything in my face anymore. And Ma…I have to go see her," he said in a daze. "So many things are beginning to fall into place now. The Pa…I always thought it was me, that I was the bad one, but really it was about him. His guilt every time he looked at me – the 'pious man', I had him on a pedestal – always trying to be like him and never succeeding." David scoffed. "I was living evidence of his weakness – his big sin."

"Go and see your mother David. Talk to her."

Chapter Nineteen

Driving slowly towards the apartment building, he remembered how his mother had protested at first about leaving the old place in her familiar neighborhood. He finally convinced her to take a look at a new building in the same area. It was one of the things that brought him the most pleasure from earning money.

The new building had an elevator, central heating and both hot and cold running water. And now that she was alone, it was all the more important that she had these conveniences. He had been so happy to do it for them even though his father never acknowledged any appreciation. The Pa was a prisoner of his pride, David realized now. His mother often told him how proud she was of him and said his father was too – he just couldn't express himself. David was skeptical about that and vowed to himself if he ever had children, they would never have to doubt his feelings for them. A thought occurred to him that he and Jorie had never talked about children or even the possibility of marriage. It seemed that working through his problems had been the main focus of their relationship and now, here was another one of 'David's problems'.

On the way, he stopped at a Kosher deli and picked up a cinnamon Danish, six white seed bagels, some cream cheese and lox. Not his favorite, but he knew his mother liked it. Stepping off the elevator on the second floor, the familiar smells of cooking wafted by his nose. Using the key he had made in case of an emergency, he unlocked the door and let himself in.

"Ma!" he yelled from the hallway so he wouldn't startle her. "It's me, David." He noted a laundry basket on the floor with freshly pressed clothes. Another perk he was glad she had. Her own washer and dryer. No more laundering everything by hand – having to heat the big kettle and pour it into the cold water tub. Those big sheets he used to help her with, dripping water across the floor as they lugged them to the clothes line in the freezing weather, their wet hands red and chapped from the cold. It calmed him to think of her warm and snug, not having to carry in wood for the stove when the gas heater wasn't strong enough on bitter winter days to heat the cold water flat. And his Ma sleeping in the room farthest from the heat, the coldest room in the flat so the kids should be warm – you could see your breath on freezing winter mornings. It had been a hard life growing up, but still, as Jorie said, it built character and he could see it made him fully appreciate the better things he was able to afford now.

Entering the kitchen, Malka had her back to him working at the stove. The place she was happiest. Her back was a little less straight, her hair was completely white and she was plumper now that she had more money for food. He was overcome with a feeling of tenderness watching her stir the pot as he had seen her do so many times. He went over and put his hands on her shoulders and whispered, "ich hub der leeb. I love you Ma."

Putting the stir spoon aside, she turned off the gas flame, "Dovey, vas is dis?" David couldn't remember ever being physically demonstrative with anyone in the family. There had been no birthday parties, no joyous occasions, so few celebrations he could count on one hand, but beatings, oh yes, and then his mother would hug and sooth him; but spontaneous hugging from love and kissing each other in greeting, never. Except for aunt Esther, who always suffocated them with kisses and Uncle Levi who would shake hands, often concealing a quarter in his palm, there was never any real show of affection. Although the roots entwined between Adam, their mother and himself, even Ruth, were strong without demonstration. Maybe his parents had never received any affection themselves growing up. They had come from hard beginnings, he knew that from Uncle Levi. *I'll have to go see uncle Levi and auntie Brunya.* He was suddenly overcome with a feeling of affection for them.

"I said, ich hub der leeb, Ma." David's eyes were moist.

Malka seeing the bright eyes said, "Kum a hare Dovey." They went into the parlor and sat down on the worn sofa, the one she had insisted on keeping from the old place.

"Is it about what Ruth said to your friend? That was a not nice thing she did and I told her."

David had only heard his mother raise her voice once in all his years, and that was at the Pa. And he couldn't remember her chastising the children, ever. Although, he thought back, there was the time when he was eleven and came home and told her he had joined up to become a junior police cadet at the police station. She carried on something terrible. 'Police? Oy! Oy! They're going to make you fight, they'll give you a gun, you'll get hurt! – why Dovey! Why would you go to the police station without asking first?' Her reaction had shaken him so badly he couldn't sleep that night. Because when she did say something critical about one's behavior, it carried a great deal of weight. He was sure Ruth hadn't taken her words lightly.

"Nu? What has got you so upset?"

"How are you doing Ma – without the Pa?"

"That's what you came to ask? I'm doing fine."

"Would you tell me if you weren't?"

"You would know."

"They caught the murderers, Ma. Two gang members of the punk the Pa injured when they broke into his pawn shop. They said it was a revenge killing. Can you imagine, after all this time? There will be a trial, but the police said they found plenty of evidence of other crimes when they raided their hang-out."

"I'm glad for that," she said quietly. They lapsed into a thoughtful silence.

No use putting off the inevitable. "Ma, I found out. I'm not yours," David blurted out in an anguished voice.

Without hesitation his mother replied, "You're not? Then whose are you?"

"Ma, you know, Adam told me the whole story."

"You mean the story about the Pa bringing me home a beautiful baby boy. An innocent, sweet baby who needed a home and love. Just like all baby's need? A baby who grew into a wonderful, caring man that has been the light of my life? You mean that story?"

David was completely taken aback. He had never seen this side of his mother. Her life had been about making ends meet, putting nourishing food on the table for her family, even when money was so short she often went to bed hungry, keeping the kids clean and neat in hand-me-downs, just the practicalities of life. She never asked for anything for herself. She never expressed an opinion on anything – she just held her nose to the grindstone and made sure the children's needs were met. He was overcome with love and a new, deeper appreciation for her.

"But Ma, I'm not Jewish... technically. Where do I fit in?"

"You are what you want to be Dovey. You're still Adam's brother. You're still my child and when Ruth gets help with her problems, you'll still be her brother."

David looked down at the toes of his shoes on the gold colored carpeting. A heavy silence hung between them while he thought about what she said. "What if I don't want to be *so* Jewish Ma?" He couldn't bring himself to look her in the face.

She reached out and took his hand in both of hers. "Dovey, the Pa wasn't always religious. After you came to me, he changed. Maybe his guilt drove him to become more strict. It wasn't good. He became a bitter man. I'm not saying he didn't have reason. He had many bad things happen that would have broken a weaker man. I let him be what he wanted to be. Could I have stopped him? No. Can someone make you religious or not religious? No. Only you know what's important to you. Keep that part of yourself you want and let go of the things you don't. The only thing that is important in this world is to be a good person. A kind person. And I know you are that. Now come, I made a pot of chicken soup this morning and I have a fresh Challah bread."

David felt his heart physically swell with love for this simple, but shockingly wise woman who sat beside him. His mother – his real mother.

He had one more question. "Ma, did you hate her? My birth-mother?"

"Hate her? Why Dovey? It was the Pa who was married, who broke his vow. If it wouldn't be her, it would have been another, nu? And besides, the gift she gave me – how could I ever hate someone who gave me such a gift?"

David felt humbled by his mother's generosity.

"Now come. Eat, you'll feel better." As they walked toward the kitchen, she touched his arm stopping him. "That girl you brought to the bris. She's nice? She's a good girl?"

"She's very nice Ma, but…"

"You'll bring her by some day. I would like to meet her."

"I'll do that." Impulsively he grasped her large gnarled hand and kissed it.

Leaving his mother's apartment, he felt the weight of the world lifted off his shoulders. Now he had to digest all this new information and sort through to what was important to him. He wanted to see Adam and tell him what a brilliant mother they both had. He wanted to see Jorie and explain all these new feelings he had inside him. He felt as if he was floating on air. There were still things he needed to unravel in his mind, but that would come over time. *Words can be so damning sometimes and so blessedly freeing at other times.* His mother's words had lifted him up and set him on a path to freedom.

He was driving back to his apartment, his mind racing – he needed to talk. Making a U-turn he drove to Jorie's building. She was just getting ready for bed when the doorbell rang. After inquiring who it was, she opened the door to see David standing there beaming from ear to ear.

"My gosh David. What happened? When I saw you last you were the picture of doom and gloom. Come in."

"Jorie," he said, picking her up and twirling her around. "Did you know I had an uncomplicated genius for a mother?" he said, putting her down and taking her hand he led her quickly into the living room.

Laughing at his excitement she said, "well, you're pretty smart and you are her son." Instantly she regretted her faux-pas. But David was on too much of an emotional high. Settling onto the sofa, he pulled her down next to him.

"Jorie, I want you to be the first to know."

"The first to know what?"

"My mother loves me."

"Was it ever in doubt? You always said you and she had a close relationship."

"Yes, but that was before I found out she wasn't my birth mother."

"But she always knew and she still loved you, and Adam even acknowledged you were her favorite."

"She said she would like to meet you."

"Really."

"Yes, really – I think things are going to work out for us."

"Whoa there, David. Rein yourself in. I gather you had a good talk with her, but there's still other members of the family, and your community, to contend with. Or are you forgetting about your lovely sister."

"Ruth has her own problems right now," he glossed over.

Jorie had never seen him so wound up. "Earth to David...I can see you're on a high, but you know what comes after? Reality. So calm down a bit please."

"I am calm – I'm just happy – it's a strange feeling and I like it!"

"Want some coffee?" she asked, starting to get up. "I have decaf."

He pulled her back down. "Let's just sit here for a few minutes. I want to share my feeling of happiness with you."

"This is so far from the brooding, self-contained David I know – I'm a little unsure of where to go with this. I mean, I'm happy that you're happy – but the kind of euphoria you're experiencing usually doesn't last."

"I've been thinking a lot about what I really care about and I definitely care about you...how can you and I explain why we have an attraction to each other? I can't answer that, but I know I have a stubborn, insecure ego that I have to work on. And what do I owe my religious community? – I have to work through that. I can't just cast off everything I've been taught – at my core, I'm Jewish, but...I've always felt I was different...I want to experience things and go places that I was always taught were not for us. 'Religion first, whatever is left-over is yours.' Only there was never anything left over. Religion and rituals ate up all my time and thinking. Does that make sense to you?"

"Yes, but I'd like you to calm down a bit," she said, grasping his hand and holding it between her two.

"I am calm. It's just that I've had an epiphany, a realization of who I am and who I want to be going forth. I will never be happy trying to live my life for others who think I should behave a certain way and condemn me if I don't. I've asked myself, when is a sacrifice worth making and when is it too much? Just because you're born into a religion…what if I had been born into the Protestant or Catholic religion, then I would have believed in their doctrine. Don't you see?"

"David, I do see, but you can't just cut off your roots…"

"I'm not cutting off my roots," he interrupted, "I'm just altering them in a different direction. I know we'll have to reckon further with my family's theological differences, but that's what relationships are about. I want us, you and me, to be united in whichever way the stakes fall. Jorie, I am deeply sorry for the way I behaved when we lived together that brief period. I know now the guilt and fear of rejection - all of it was crushing me and I didn't know how to deal with it."

"And now you do? Or think you do?"

He gave her a rueful look. "I think my mind is in a better place and whatever I have to deal with, I would like it if you were by my side. If we could work together towards a united front."

"And your birth-mother? Are you interested in finding out more about her?"

"I thought about that too. What would be the advantage? As far as I know, there were no other children and truthfully, I can't imagine anyone, even if she was still alive, replacing the mother I've been lucky enough to have."

Jorie found herself deeply touched by the bond David felt with his mother. She marveled at it and it made her question her own relationship with her parents. She vowed to stop taking them for granted and appreciate all the gifts of the good life they had given her – think of them as people – *we always talk, but have I really heard what they say? Or have I only been interested in my own goals?*

"Jorie, I want us to get married."

"Married?" she exclaimed pulling in her chin. "Oh my god! I wasn't expecting this."

"Not right now. First I need to work on myself. Let go of my anger and guilt. I can do it, because I want us to be happy and to experience all that life has to offer, together. I feel that I have finally freed my spirit and now I want to laugh and bury the guilt… not inside me," he quickly added before she could respond. I think we should have a 'guilt burning' ceremony. What do you think?"

"I, I don't know, I've never been to one. Is it a Jewish thing?"

David laughed. "No, but I'm going to write down everything that I ever felt guilty for and we'll set the paper on fire and all the guilt will float away as it turns to ashes."

"Who are you and what have you done with 'dour David'?"

"I think 'dour David' has left the body. From now on I'm going to be 'happy David', able to cope with whatever comes my way and Jorie, I love you with all my heart. Stick with me and we're going to have a good life, I can promise you that." He grabbed her arms and pulled her close nuzzling her neck.

"Just one more thing. Is there a silly David somewhere in there? Let me hear you laugh; I want to experience silly happy David."

"You want to hear me laugh? Okay, but be prepared." He started making loud laughing noises **Hahahahahah** and then morphed into braying like a donkey, until Jorie found herself convulsing with laughter holding her stomach.

Shaking her head, she said, "I promise to always love you dour David, happy David, silly David, whoever or whatever you are today. We'll find a way to make it work this time."

Epilogue

October 14, 2020

11:30 PM. A body hit the floor – the sound was unmistakable. Threw down my book and raced up the stairs. Face down, naked, unconscious, hands at his sides, his head against the bed frame bent at an odd angle, a pool of blood spreading rapidly outward. 911!

"Wake up!". Hitting his back. The operator asking questions. Focus! "Yes, yes! We're both healthy. Until five minutes ago we were both healthy! Where's the ambulance?"

"They're on your doorstep now."

Throw phone onto the bed. Fly down the stairs to unlock the door. The dog is barking; trying to corral him into a bathroom. The ambulance people are bringing equipment in. "Upstairs!" Grab hold of Beaver's collar. He slips it. Caught his tail. Scooped him up. Like trying to pick up a god-damn slinky toy! Dragged him into a room and shut the door. My feet pounding back upstairs. Medic bandaging his head. I hear him, "low blood pressure." Stench! Expelled bowels. Throwing up. They're moving him.

"He's going to live isn't he?" I hear pleading.

Outside, the fire truck. First responders. An ambulance at the curb. People. I see nothing except the stretcher being loaded into the ambulance and his pale face. Cell phone! Here! I thrust it at the attendant. He's driven away. I can't go with him. Damn Covid!

1:30 AM – I finish the clean-up and fall into bed. The adrenalin overload is draining away. A big tiredness over-comes me but I can't sleep. Memories like bee stings float in and out. What a rocky path we trod. How naive I was. How angry he had been. But we muddled through it and it made our bond even stronger. Fifty-two years together through all the ups and downs. When am I going to hear anything?!

7:20 AM - Ring – I pick up the phone.

Thank you to my good friends for all your support and feedback…

Debbie Temperton – the best, most wonderfully upbeat normal human being a person could want for a friend.

Claudia Donovan – Thank you for your encouragement. It means more than you can know.

Gail Gamache – my sister and my friend.

Arlyle Waring – Your enthusiasm and creativity give me wings.

Lorraine Green – just because you're you.

Abe Coisman – My handsome forever man, through thick and thin.

Patricia resides in Montreal with her husband Abe and enthusiastic dog, Benji.

Until she retired from the art business to write novels, Patricia was a professional artist who had several successful solo exhibitions and toured Canada and the United States selling her art. Her paintings were featured in many magazines, books and catalogs and she was the recipient of multiple awards. Most recently featured in the December, 2021 issue of Costco magazine.

To learn more, you can visit her websites www.patriciabourque.com or www.patriciabourque.net

Made in the USA
Middletown, DE
25 March 2024